"UNDERCOVER SECRETS"

BY:

RITA GAMBINO & GIOVANNI GAMBINO

A Club Lighthouse Publishing E-Book

ISBN: 978-1-927337-38-7

All rights reserved

Copyright © 2012 Rita Gambino and Giovanni Gambino

Registration Number
TXu- 001-798-845

Copyrighted 2012-03-01

Cover Art: T.L. Davison 2012

For information contact:

comments@clublighthousepublishing.com

A Club Lighthouse Memoir Edition
Published in Canada

DEDICATION

This Book is dedicated

To the

Memory

Of

Francesco Gambino
Jan 2, 1941 to Jan 4, 2012

CHAPTER ONE

"DO I NEED TO SHOOT the door down or will you come out of the bathroom willingly?" Nikki was getting restless waiting for her husband to get out of the bathroom.

"Oh, take it easy there killer, what's the big rush?" Brian came out of the bathroom with both hands up.

Nikki punched her husband in the stomach. "You know better than to fuck with a woman Fed." Brian held his stomach from the blow his wife gave him. "I'll tell you one thing; they got the right gal for the job, that's for sure."

She smiled and walked into the bathroom. 'So, what's the big rush?" Nikki was in the bathroom rushing because she didn't want to be late; "I'm getting my new assignment today."

"Oh yeah anyone good?"

"Oh come on, you know if I tell you I will have to kill you."

"Come on honey it's me, your husband." She hesitated and before replying; "Luca Marchisio". Brian stopped dead in his tracks, "WHAT?"

Nikki peeked her head out of the bathroom, repeating; "I said Luca Marchisio." "I heard what you said, Nikki are they nuts? This is the biggest gangster out there." She rolled her eyes as she put on her shirt. "I know I'm so excited."

"Nikki, I'm a little nervous about this."

"Why? They are not asking you to do the job."

"I know, but you are dealing with big gangsters here and the thought of something happening to you, scares the shit out of me."

Nikki stopped, putting her hands on Brian's face; "Brian you knew about my job before we got married and that it will be a big part of my life, so now you have to deal with it."

Brian grabbed Nikki by the waist and pulled her close. "I love you honey and I want you around for a long time."

"I love you too but I have to go to work, so suck it up and be a man. Don't worry about me, I'm a big girl and no one fucks with Nikki Jacobs. Anyway, don't be so worried. My job is to stay in the van and keep tabs on him. Remember I'm the brains of this operation. I say when, who and how."

Brian smiled at Nikki; "and they picked the right person for it."

"Honey, I love to sit here and chit chat, but I'm really excited about getting this started."

Brian gave Nikki a big kiss "I love you, please be careful."

"I always am."

CHAPTER TWO

LUCA MARCHISIO WAS A gangster who was just being released from prison. He had done time for the family; took the rap and refused to turn anyone in. Luca took his job and oath very seriously. He hated anyone who tried fucking with the family. Luca's thing was "FUCK THEM", to anyone who crossed or betrayed the family. Mr. Buoncuore was the boss. He had raised Luca as his own son. Mr. B and Luca's dad were best friends so when he was killed, Mr. B took care of Luca. So Luca was not going to betray his family after all they had done for him, and he did the four years with pride.

"Vin, I forgot how great the sun feels beating on my face and the wind blowing in my hair."

"Luca, what the fuck, did you turn gay in prison?"

"Vin, you ever say gay and my name in the same sentence I will fucking kill you."

"I'm kidding, jerk off, a few years in prison will do that to you. So Luca how was it?"

"What?"

"You know being locked up."

"Oh Vin, it was a party every day, we had girls come and got fucking laid every night. Take out dinners, it was fucking amazing."

"Really?"

"Vin, how the fuck do you think it was? It was fucking hell."

"What did you do in there?"

"I read a lot; I got a lot of inspiration in there. I was actually thinking of writing about my experience."

"Ok Luca, now you are a writer?"

"Why not?"

"I'll tell you why, because word on the street is that they are thinking of making you the next top dog."

"Really, who told you that?"

"Well, we were all out last night and the boss was saying how proud he was of you for not opening your mouth. You know you could've fucked us all."

"Vin, I'm no fucking rat! I took an oath and I honor every word of that oath. I'm actually a little insulted that he would think that I would turn on my family."

"Luca listen, nowadays it's the big guys that are turning rats, not the little ones. Maybe that's why he thought that." Luca rolled his eyes and looked away, "well I'm no small guy." Vinny all serious looked at his buddy with concern, "listen Luca, the boss wants to see you."

"Now?"

"No, go home shower, relax a little. Maybe you want to call one of your bimbos and get laid; you know four years is four years. Then come tonight around seven at the usual spot." Luca looked all annoyed; he didn't feel like a meeting tonight. "Is Mickey's still the usual spot?"

"Of course it is, where else would we go?"

"Who the fuck knows, I've been out of the loop for four years. I can't meet him tonight I have a meeting with this huge producer."

"Producer, what the fuck are you talking about?"

"I met this kid in prison, his uncle is a major producer and he thinks I'm perfect for his uncle's new movie."

Vinny was shocked and very confused, "Luca, you don't say no to the boss. What the fuck did they do to you in there?"

"Vin, its better I don't see them tonight, you know how many fucking eyes are on me right now? Anyway, what if we did things different, why can't we make money this way, with the entertainment business, movies and books. Why the fuck does everything have to be illegal?" Vinny shook his head in disbelief, "what the fuck do you want me to tell the boss?"

"Just tell him that I just got out, it's for both of our benefits to stay away today. Tell him I'm hooking up with some broads and getting fucking laid! What the fuck Vin, do I have to teach you everything! How many years have we been best friends?"

"Our whole lives."

"Right so you know what you have to tell him. Tell him I'll meet him tomorrow."

"What if—"

Luca stopped him, "Vin, if nothing? I'm not meeting him tonight. I need my day, I just fucking got out."

"Ok Luca, I'll call you if anything—"

"Ok that will work." Luca, got out of the car, shook Vinny's hand, "thanks buddy for picking me up."

"Are you fucking kidding, if I didn't who would've?"

"What you saying, I have no friends?"

"No jerk off, I'm your best friend, I missed you man." Vinny looked at Luca with a smirk, "ok now whose gay?"

"Goodbye Vin, don't forget what I told you." Vinny, pulled away and took off.

* * * * *

NIKKI WAS RUNNING LATE, she got out of the office and went straight to the van to see what was going on. She knocked three times on the door of the van. Larry and George were in there already listening to Luca. "What's going on guys", what do we have so far?"

"Nothing yet, Vinny just dropped him off and he just got to his apartment."

"Ok good, did we bug everything like I told you?"

"Yes, we got the bedroom, kitchen, living room and bathroom."

"Great, so now we know when he's taking a shit. George laughed, "Really, did we have to do that? That's kind of gross."

"George, let me ask you something when you are talking to your girlfriend and you don't want your wife to hear you where do you go?"

"In the bathroom."

"Ok so shut up and sit down." Larry interrupted the two of them, "he's making a call."

"Yeah, Mark it's me, Luca."

"Hey Luca how are you, you finally got out?"

"Yeah I just got out, just walked in to be exact. Listen I'm really glad you decided to meet me tonight. When your nephew told me you thought I was perfect for the part, I was a little excited."

"Yeah I'm excited too; I think you will be perfect to play the part. So then the audition for the movie is at seven?"

"Yes meet me at my office, 325 Park Avenue. Ok, so thanks again for this opportunity to star in your movie, I'll see you later."

Nikki stopped, looking at Larry and George, "what the fuck was that," who the fuck is Mark? George, I asked you to do one thing, your job was to bug his apartment."

"I did"!

"Then what the fuck was that?" Larry looked at the both of them,

"Are you guys ever going to get along?"

They both responded at the same time, "NO"!

"Ok listen, apparently Luca had this inspiration in prison; he got into books and movies. One of the kids in prison set him up with an audition for this big movie."

Nikki was confused while Larry was making his prediction,

"Wait a minute, so you are telling me he's an actor, what did they do to him in prison? What, did he turn gay? Here I am all excited about this big case and he's a fucking actor? WHERE THE FUCK IS MY GANGSTER? Ok let me think. George, I need you to go to this office and plant a bug. Maybe this is just double talk and he figures he's being bugged, being that he just got out. So go to the office as a tech and plant a bug, I want to hear this meeting tonight."

George looked at Nikki, surprised, "Now?"

"Yeah now! Larry you stay here, keep listening and tell me if anything comes in. I have to go meet with the chief. I want to know what the fuck is going on. Luca Marchisio an actor? What is this, a joke? Don't they know what they will do to him if they find out? Ok guys get to it. I'm sure he's going to take a shower and just relax until his meeting. Larry, I'll meet you at 325 Park, keep in touch with me."

"Ok boss, will do."

Nikki got into her car and took off. She was so pissed, *how can they do this to me? My biggest case and the gangster turns soft on me? This is an insult; they know I'm better than this.* She pulled into the station and left the car with a mission. As she was walking through the station everyone could see that she was pissed off.

"Hey Nikki, I heard your gangster turned actor overnight."

"Mike, I see news travels fast around here."

Mike and a few of the other guys started to laugh. This pissed Nikki off even more.

"Don't worry boys; I will have the last laugh."

She knocked on the chief's door.

"Come in Nikki."

"Chief what is this? Some kind of a joke?"

"What are you talking about Nikki?"

"Really? You don't know?"

"Yes I heard, so what's the problem?"

"It's supposed to be my biggest case and you turn it into a three ring circus?"

"Nikki, how am I supposed to know that he would grow a conscience in prison? Listen, you don't know what's going on yet, go and listen to this meeting."

"You have me following a dead beat here. How am I supposed to bust all of them if I am running around listening to this so called "gangster" audition for movies?"

"Nikki, word on the street is that he's the next big man, so you need to follow him and see where he takes you. This could all be a cover for something big. Come on Nikki, what do you think they will do to him once they find out what he's doing? You are my smartest and best officer here, that's why I made you the brains of this operation. I know you can get them all, I have faith in you"

"Fine, I will put up with this, for now but know this; I will not be taken for a fool. I'm too good for this and you know it"

"Yes I do, and that's why you are my TOP dog."

Nikki smiled and walked out of the office. Everyone was listening, and when she walked out, they all turned and made believe that they were working.

"Nikki, so what is he auditioning for?" Mike was laughing at Nikki and poking fun at her. Nikki walked over to Mike, getting really close to him and she put her arms around his neck in a very sexy seductive tone she whispers in his ear; "my lover!" Mike just stood there with his mouth opened. She walked away and Mike couldn't help but turn and watch her every move as she walked out of the office. Nikki was a very beautiful woman; not your typical Fed. She was very tall, slender and fit, she was all legs. She had long golden brown hair and the most beautiful piercing green eyes. So every man in the squad room would've loved to be with her. But Nikki was tough she was no typical girly girl. She didn't take shit from anyone. She was there to prove a point; that a woman can take out the mob. Something that none of them were able to do. This was her mission, her goal. When she walked out, all eyes were on her.

Peter turned to Mike; "She told you Mike?"

"Yeah, she wants me."

"In your dreams Mike."

"And she's in them every night."

CHAPTER 3

LUCA WAS GETTING READY for his meeting with the producer when his phone rang.

"Talk to me"

"Hey Luca, its Vin"

"Vin, what's the word?"

"I spoke to the boss; he's fine with you taking the night off and was very impressed of how you thought of the family, knowing that they probably are on your tail. But he wants to meet with you early tomorrow for breakfast at his house"

"Ok, no problem, tell him I'll be there."

"Hey Luca, what if you get this part?"

"Then I will be a big star."

"Yeah but Lu, what the fuck is the family going to think? They won't have a big man like you doing movies; too many eyes will be around you. You can't let them know you are doing this"

"Vin, listen to me, don't worry about it, I'll take care of everything. I have everything under control. You just keep your mouth shut and just be there when I need you."

"You know I always am."

"Hey Lu, good luck on your audition."

"Thanks bro; I'll call you after."

* * * * *

NIKKI WAS JUST GETTING to the van when Larry called her.

"Nikki, I got news for you, where are you?"

"I'm right outside the van, open up. What's up?"

"He's got a meeting tomorrow with the boss at the house."

"Oh good, at last some action."

"Where is George?"

"He's heading down now; he had some problems getting in."

"Why?"

"He wasn't on the list and he had to work around it and finally got in."

"Do we have confirmation that it works?"

"Yes, I heard the assistant say to Mr. Borotolli that Luca was waiting for him." Just as they were finishing up their conversation, George knocked on the van door.

"Boy, I'm good."

Nikki looked at George and smacked him off the head; "Really? If you were that good you would know that you had to get on the list before you walked in the building."

"Honey, why do you always have to knock me down?"

"Don't honey me George."

"I forgot I lost that right after we broke up." George and Nikki used to date. They were together for a while but George never told her he was married. Nikki was very set against being the other woman, so when they broke up, it didn't end well. She was still sour even though it was three years ago. She wasn't that crazy about him being on her team but she had every intention to make this experience a living hell for him.

"George, sit down and shut the fuck up."

"Oh baby are you pmsing today?"

"One more remark out of your mouth and I'll put you on coffee duty."

"Yeah, you're pmsing."

"That's it, get out! Go out and get me a mocha, I need my fix."

"Yes, and I know exactly how you like it. Larry, coffee?"

"No, I'm good, thanks"

George walked out; "I'm in the mood for coffee anyway."

"Yeah take your time, don't rush back."

Nikki turned to Larry; "why does he have to be so annoying?"

"Nikki, come on, are you serious?"

"What?"

"He still has the hots for you."

"Yeah, well he better go take a cold shower cause this train left the station a long time ago."

Larry motioned to Nikki; "Shhhh, he's in the office." Nikki put the headphones on and started to listen.

"Luca, it's so nice to see you again. Thanks Mark, same here. How was your day? Good, it was great to finally take a shower without all these guys staring at you."

Mark chuckled, "I'm sure it is. You sure are one hot guy."

"Mark, you are making me nervous."

"No, I'm all good. So, tell me what do you think of the book? Did you read it?"

"Yes, I did. I loved it. It had me laughing the whole time. Yes, we came across this book about a year ago, Mulberry to Rome. My nephew spoke very highly of it. He said Uncle Mark you have to read this, it's hysterical. So I did, and I thought it would make a great comedy. So now here we are turning it into a movie. It really is amazing how the author has the gangsters going back to Roman times and meeting Cesar. And who knew, that's how we got Cesar salad."

They both laughed.

"I want you to play the lead gangster; I think you have the looks, the wits and the smarts for it." "Yeah sure Mark whatever you want; when do you want me to audition?"

"Really, I'm set on you and I know your character; I'm pretty much giving you the part."

"Oh wow, that's great so I already have the part?"

"Yeah, I had you in mind from our first meeting when I went to see my nephew. You had me laughing with all your gangster stories and I knew you were 'it'."

"Well, I'm flattered, thank you."

Listen, we are just working on the other actors, we should be starting in a few weeks. I'm sure you want a little break before you start working again."

"Yeah but I'm ready, I've been in a cell for four years. I need to do something."

"Well, I'm sure you have a lot of catching up to do with your 'family'."

"Yes, I do. Just between you and me, right now let's keep this on the down low. I have to work 'The Family' first. I have to find a way of making them see this as a good thing."

"Oh, I hear you Luca. Just be careful, we are shooting in a few weeks and I mean the movie."

Luca laughed at his horrible humour. "Yeah I'm always careful. Ok then so we have a deal and I will keep in touch and let you know when to come in."

"No problem Mark; thanks again."

"Oh no Luca, thank you, I think you are going to be a hit on the big screen." They shook hands and Luca walked out.

Nikki just looked at Larry,

"What is he thinking? Did he really lose his mind? What is the family going to think about this? This will be too much attention to the family"

"I don't know Nikki, maybe he wants out?" Nikki gave Larry a crazy look,

"Larry no one ever gets out unless they are six feet under. He's going to get himself killed." Nikki just looked at him as he was walking out of the building, "Luca what are you doing?" And it was like he knew they were there, because he looked right at the van and for the first time, she saw him and thought; *he is a very good looking guy.*

Luca was also very tall and built. He had this aura about him; he was fine and very handsome. He always dressed very well and had ways with his words. Nikki had read up on him when they first told her she would be working on his case once he got out. He always seemed to be one of the good guys, trying to keep peace between the families. He hated rats more than anything. He couldn't stand people who turned on the family. His motto was; *"You are a rat, you're done, fuck him."* He hated violence. He felt if they can talk it out, less people would die. Nikki was very impressed by this so when she finally put the face with the subject, she found herself liking him. She shook that thought right out of her mind. "Larry, follow him home; don't leave him unless I say so. I have my car so I'm going to the station to do some research. Listen, if you see that he's not doing anything just call me; there's no reason for you to stick around but I will see you in the morning at the boss's house." Just as she was walking out of the van, George was walking in with the coffee.

"Hey, where are you going?"

"Where did you go, to Colombia to pick the beans?"

"You are so funny Nikki."

"Yeah didn't you know; I work stand up part time. Thanks for the coffee, see you in the morning"

"So no dinner?"

"With you, I don't think so."

"Oh baby you hurt me so much."

"Yeah you haven't seen anything yet."

She got in her car and left. When she got to the squad room and it was pretty empty, everyone had called it a night. However, she wanted to know about this book, this movie that they were making. *Maybe there's some hidden message in this book.* She had to get her hands on it. As she was searching the web she saw these two goons walk in.

"Can I help you?"

"We are looking for Mike."

"I don't think he's here, I believe everyone left for the night."

"Oh no he's here, he's waiting for us."

Nikki was a little taken back, *who are these guys and why are they coming here at this hour of the night?* Mike walked out and was a little surprised to see Nikki at her desk working.

"Mike these guys are here for you, you know them?"

"Yeah that's Paul and Joe; they are working on something for me. Guys, go to the back, I'll be there in a minute."

"Yeah no problem Mike. Who's the babe? You banging her?"

Mike laughed, "Yeah she wishes."

"Excuse me?" Nikki got up and went right for Mike.

"Take it easy, I'm kidding."

"She's a feisty one Mike."

"Yeah you have NO IDEA."

Nikki looked at Mike; "What are you working on Mike?"

"It's nothing major, just a small case on a drug bust. These guys just came in from Canada; I need them to do stuff for me."

"They look like gangsters."

"Yeah they are on the payroll, hey what's with all the questions?"

"I'm a Fed, that's my job."

"What are you still doing here?"

"I'm looking for this book, Mulberry to Rome."

"Oh yeah, that book was hysterical."

"You read it?"

"Yeah I did, it was funny; it's a fiction."

"Where can I get a copy?"

"Anywhere, I got it at the Barnes and Nobles down the block."

"You think they are still open?"

"Nikki, it's 11:30 PM, no, I doubt they are opened. Why don't you go home and get some rest? You had a long day."

Nikki just looked at Mike with suspicion, *why does he want me to leave so bad?*

"Yeah, I think you're right, I have a long day ahead of me and I want to go get this book."

"Ok then, have a good night."

"You too Mike."

* * * * *

I T WAS A LITTLE PAST midnight when Nikki got home. Brian was already in bed but watching TV. He heard her walk in; "now there's my big boss woman." She just gave him a look of disgust; "please don't even get me started." Brian jumped out of bed and went to her,

"What happened honey? Was it not all you thought it would be?"

"Oh Brian, you know I can't really discuss my case with you."

"I know, but it's me."

"As much as I wish I could, I really can't. I told you who I was watching and that was more than I need to tell you."

"Nikki, I'm your husband and I worry. You are not dealing with every day little criminals, you are dealing with the mob!"

"Yeah thanks for the update, you don't need to remind me."

She sat on the couch and Brian started rubbing her shoulders.

"Oh I can get used to this." She sighed.

"Honey you are so tense, let me help you release some of that stress."

"That sounds like an amazing idea but I am so tired that I can't even function."

"You don't have to do anything, just lay there."

"OK well you know me too well, I can't just lay there."

"That's right, I forgot who I was talking too, the one who is always in control; my boss woman."

"Honey, don't call me that, it sounds really corny."

She turned around to look at him and he was standing there in his boxers and no shirt. Brian was a very attractive man, he was built. He was tall with light brown hair and hazel eyes. He was a fireman. They met 3 years ago at a government party; his engine was named the number one group for the year. She was actually George's date at the time. Brian's party was part of that engine. They just hit it off from the beginning. She was very attracted to him and the fact that she loved firemen helped a little. After she broke things off with George, he came around looking for her and they had been together ever since. They were married 2 years and Brian wanted children, but in her line of work that was a little hard. She was still young, and wasn't ready.

"Baby, when are we going to make a baby? With my looks and your brains, this kid is going to be amazing."

"What are you saying I'm not good looking?"

"Nikki, you are hot"!

"So then?"

"I'm just saying, OK, I see you are not in the mood for this."

"No Brian I am not, I'm really tired but I will tell you this, I promise you after this case is over I will be ready to have a baby."

"Really? You mean it?"

"Yes, I think I'm ready to be a mommy."

"I love you baby."

"I love you too."

"Ok listen, go to bed and maybe we can start tomorrow."

She laughed and agreed. She tried to sleep but couldn't. She just kept seeing Luca. *Why is this man in my head? I know he's my subject right now but I've never lost sleep over a case before, not like this.* She kept picturing him coming out of the building, walking to his car and looking so handsome.

"Oh my God, get out of my head!"

"Baby, are you ok?"

She didn't realize how loud she said that, it woke Brian up.

"I'm sorry, I was having a nightmare. I'm ok, go back to sleep."

She got up and started to look at his file again, this time she was just flipping through his pictures. *He really is a good looking guy. Why didn't I ever see that before? Ok I need to just snap out of it and go to bed. It's like when he looked at me from the van, we connected somehow, but how is that even possible? He couldn't have seen me.* She was thinking she was losing her mind. She made herself some Chamomile tea and went to bed.

CHAPTER 4

Nikki WAS UP AND out early the next day, she didn't even wake Brian up. She kissed him while he was sleeping and said a very low I love you and walked out. She didn't waste any time at all, and was dialing Larry as she was walking out of the house.

"Larry, what do you have for me, any news?"

"Nah, he was pretty quiet last night, some girl went up there and he was at it for hours."

"And you listened? I know George would but you?"

Larry laughed out loud; "He had a lot of frustration to get out."

"Spare me the details please. Where are you now?"

"We are at his place waiting for him. Vinny is picking him up in a few minutes"

"Ok, I'm on my way. I'll meet you at the boss's house."

"Sounds good Nikki."

Nikki was driving and thinking at the same time; *what if there is something in that book, a hidden message of some kind? There's no way he's turning soft. He's a gangster for god sake; they don't read books or want to be in movies. Maybe read playboy and watch porn, but to be in a movie or write a book? Something is definitely up and I'm going to get to the bottom of it.* She was by the Buoncuore Estate. She couldn't park too close, so she parked about two blocks away. She was just admiring the Estate. It truly was an amazing house. White beautiful house set up on top of the hill, surrounded with trees for privacy and big golden gates at the entrance with bodyguards and cameras everywhere. *Blood money, how can people live like that after knowing how many people and lives they ruined?* She was disgusted by it.

Tomasso Buoncuore, also known has Mr. B., was the head of the family. He was climbing up there in age and was looking to retire. He had no sons, just daughters. Three beautiful, spoiled girls, who knew exactly how to get what they wanted from their daddy, He was very attached to Luca; he was like the son he never had. And especially after taking the rap for him and doing time for the family, he knew it was Luca who was going to take his place. He tried to set him up with one of his daughters but Luca never liked to mix business with pleasure. This was a very big meeting and Nikki couldn't wait to put her earphones on and listen.

* * * * *

"YO! LUCA, WHAT THE fuck you doing up there? Come on already, you are going to be late."

"I'm coming, relax yourself and lower your fucking voice; I have neighbors who sleep in the morning. Who were you raised by? A bunch of wolves?"

"Yeah, pretty much."

"What a wise ass you are Vin."

"Look at you Lu, all sharp in that nice suit. Where you think you going?"

Luca lightly slapped Vinny in the face, "Vin, I'm going to be a big star, I have to start looking the part."

"Yeah Luca but a suit?"

"Do you see me wearing a tie? No; so its business casual, now shut up and drive, I'm going to be late."

"You look more relaxed this morning."

"Of course I do, I finally got laid after four years in the joint."

"You lucky dog you. How was she?"

"I don't kiss and tell Vin, but I feel bad for her today. She's not going to be able to walk for days."

Vinny looked at his friend, "That's my boy"

"Vin, listen to this idea. What do you think about me writing a book on my experience in the joint?"

"Oh my god Luca, you are making me nervous with this shit. You are looking to get yourself killed."

"Why do you keep saying that?"

"You write a book, you have to say a lot of criminating shit, these Feds, they are not stupid they read into every little thing. They put events and names together and bang we all get fucking busted because of your stupid book."

"Ok, you were the wrong person to ask."

"Who else would you ask besides me? You got a new best friend while you were in the joint? YO! Luca you cheating on me?"

"Vin, listen you need to stop with all this gay shit because I will have to shoot you. And just for the record, it's only you babe! You can't be replaced."

"I thought so."

They both laughed as they were pulling into the driveway. Vinny pressed the intercom,

"Yeah who is it?"

"Vinny and Luca."

"Come right in."

"I don't get it, they have the fucking cameras can't they see who the fuck it is?"

"Shut up Luca, what do you want to do, get us killed?"

"Vin, when did you become such a pussy? Snap out of it. Four years without me and you are walking around like a scared little girl."

"Yeah, and you come out thinking you can go and win an Emmy!"

"You want my autograph now?"

"You're a dick Luca, no talk of this shit when we get inside."

"Oh, but since when do you call me a dick? Watch that mouth will you. Don't worry about what I'm going to talk about."

* * * * *

NIKKI WALKED QUICKLY TO the van, she wanted to hear everything.

"Boys, did I miss anything yet?" Larry looked at Nikki with a big smile.

"No they just walked in. Look at you. You're like a kid in a candy store."

"Are you kidding? This is why I became a Fed."

"Baby doll I got you a mocha."

"George not even you can ruin this moment for me, but thanks for the coffee."

George put out his lips for a kiss and Nikki just left him a hanging.

"Cold hearted bitch!"

"Yeah, and don't you forget it you cheating lying son of a bitch."

"Ok you got me, enough."

"Yeah, I thought so. Why are you on my team?"

"Because I paid off the chief, I wanted to make sure your first big bust would be with me standing right next you."

"George, go for a walk will you?"

"No, I'm not missing this."

"Then shut up and keep your stupid comments to yourself."

"Yes boss."

Larry waved them to shut up; "Ok guys they are in, let the meeting begin."

* * * * *

THE BOYS WALKED up to the front door.

"Luca you really do look sharp."

"Thanks bro, I really appreciate that, now stop looking at me before I slap you."

They were laughing as the youngest daughter, Maria answered the door. Maria, was eighteen, very pretty with blonde hair and blue eyes but a little on the short side. Luca liked his women tall and all legs.

"Hey guys how are you?"

"Maria, how you been?"

"Luca? OH MY GOD, Daddy didn't tell me you got out."

"Yeah I got out yesterday." She gave him a huge hug and kiss. Maria was the flirt of the family. She flirted with all the guys who worked for her father. She was also the prettiest and the only one not married yet. She had a huge crush on Luca but she was too young for him, plus he didn't mix business with pleasure. As they were walking in, Maria pulled Luca back; "you know my room is the third on the right?"

Luca gave her a smile, "Yeah, that won't be happening. Sorry no offence you're a beautiful girl but you know me, I don't date the boss' girls."

She lowered her eyes, "What a shame, I can really rock your world."

Luca just laughed and walked away. They walked into the office and Mr. B was sitting there reading the paper, drinking his coffee.

"Boys, come in, come in." He got up and walked over to Luca; "Luca my boy, how are you?" He gave him a big hug of gratitude.

"I'm good Mr. B."

"I have to tell you Luca, what you did for the family is amazing. I don't think anyone would've done what you did."

"Mr. B if I had to, I'd do it again."

"You see that's loyalty, he should've been my son", he gave him another big hug. "Sit down boys we have a lot to talk about. Luca, I know I didn't come to see you but under the circumstances, you knew I couldn't."

"Of course boss, I know that."

"I've had a lot of issues with my health, in and out of the hospitals; Vinny told you all this, no?"

"Yeah, Vin filled me in when he could. How are you feeling now boss? You doing better?"

"Yeah but you know this job of ours takes a lot out of me. With my health, I don't know how much longer I can keep doing this. This is why I have you boys here today. My time as boss is coming to an end."

"Boss, what are you saying?"

"No, nothing bad Luca, just that I think it's time to step down and give someone else a chance at all this. Now as you know, I have no sons; just my girls. Loretta and Victoria are married and their husbands are useless, they do nothing for me. My Maria, well let's not talk about my Maria, she has issues but she's young yet. Luca, you sure you don't want to marry her?"

"Boss, no offence to your daughter, she's a beautiful girl but you know how I feel about that."

"Yes, I do, Vin, what about you?"

"I'm with Luca on that, I can't date the boss' daughter."

"Anyway, the point is I have no sons. You Luca have been the closest thing I have to a son. You do a lot for me and the family and I appreciate that, and to show you my appreciation I have planned two things: One is to throw a big party, now that you're out, we need to celebrate. So in your honor this weekend we are having a huge party here at the house with all the families. Everyone needs to know what loyalty is and what a great man you truly are. Two, I've decided that I want you to take my place as boss."

"WHAT? Boss, are you serious, me, boss?"

"Yes, I think I've taught you all you need to know and you are a smart man, I know you can do the job."

"But Mr. B, I thought you were going to make me under boss, not boss."

"Well, that's where Vinny comes in, Vin I want you to be his under boss. You two are a great team and you can't separate that. I watched you boys grow into men and like any father, I'm very proud. Luca, your father and I were best friends, just like you and Vinny. We did everything together and when he died, God rest his soul, I promised him that I would take care of you as my own. And have I lived up to that promise?"

"Of course you have that and more."

"Ok then, I can't imagine anyone else doing this but you. And Vin, I want you to be his right hand man, just like you have been doing all your life." Vinny was shocked, he had no clue he was even considered for this job.

"Boss I am honored that you feel this way, I really had no clue." Luca looked at Mr. Buoncuore, "Boss, what will you be doing?"

"I will be here Luca, I will be watching you and guiding you and making sure you don't fuck up or get yourself killed. I will help you come to your decisions, I will not tell you what to do but you are a smart man, you know what you have to do. I'll be somewhat your *consigliore.*"

Luca and Vinny just looked at each other in shock.

"Ok boys, that's it for now, I will be making this huge announcement Saturday at your welcome home party. So rest up enjoy your time out because after Saturday, you will be in charge. You need anything Luca, some money, a new place to live?"

"No Mr. B, I'm all set."

"Ok, so go enjoy and listen, let's keep this quiet, I want to tell everyone Saturday."

"Yeah, sure whatever you want boss."

"That's my boys."

Mr. Buoncuore got up, hugged them both and shook their hands.

"Luca, you're looking sharp."

"Thanks Mr. B, I guess four years of rest did me some good." They all laughed and Mr. Buoncuore walked the boys out.

*   *   *   *   *

NIKKI WAS IN SHOCK, she looked at Larry with the biggest smile from ear to ear.

"Did I just hear that right? He's making him the head of the family? Oh my god, here I am thinking he's making him under boss but now I'm dealing with the big dog?"

Larry nodded and smiled, "You see Nikki, you might just get that wish of busting them all."

"Might? Oh no Larry, I am very determined to bring them all down. This has to be the happiest day of my life."

George was very happy for her. He knew what this meant to her.

"Good job boss."

"Oh George you can tell me that when they are all behind bars. Ok guys listen to me; I need to check some things out so you go back to the station. Work on all this, type it up, go over it make sure it's what we heard. Bring the chief up to speed. I will meet you at the station later."

"But Nikki, what about following Luca?"

"I'm sure they are going to lunch, they are shocked themselves. They need time to soak this all in. So do I, I just feel my load just got a lot heavier. See you boys later."

"Ok boss, touch base with us, ok?"

"Of course"

Nikki walked out of the van and practically skipped to her car. She was a pig in shit; it was like she just hit the mother lode. Nothing could bring her down today. She got in her car and headed straight to the Barnes and Noble, now she had to get the book. *There's no way he's becoming the boss and working in films. The family will totally disown him, actually they probably kill him.* So she had to get that book, she had to see what hidden message was there. As she pulled up to the book store her phone rang, it was the chief.

"Hey Nikki, I just heard the good news."

"I know. Can you believe that? Who knew what was in store for him?"

"I know, so now you need to step up your game. Be careful and don't let him out of your sight. Where are you now? I had to make a pit stop but I should be in the office shortly."

"Ok come and see me first thing."

"No problem; will do." She hung up and walked into the store.

* * * * *

LUCA AND VINNY WERE still trying to absorb all that went down at the meeting.

"Holy shit Luca, can you believe what just went down?"

"Shhhh, I want to enjoy this a little more."

"LUCA!"

"What? Relax yourself Vin, what did you expect?"

"Under boss, are you kidding Luca?"

"Who else was the old man going to name his successor, Joe balls? Of course it was going to be me. I'm the right man for the job. He knows what he's doing. I did four years for the man, if he didn't name me head boss, I would be a little pissed off."

"Yeah, but Luca me, under boss?"

"Bro, you're my right hand man, if he didn't name you under boss, I would've eventually."

"Lu you're the best."

"Yeah and don't you forget it." They got into the car.

"Vin let me drive."

"Yeah sure boss whatever you want."

"I kind of like the sound of that, say it again."

"Boss."

"Yeah, I can get used to that. Get in the car; I have to make a pit stop."

They pulled up to the book store. Luca parked the car and was about to get out. Vinny just looked at him confused, "What the fuck are we doing here?"

"Vin, what are you waiting for an invitation? Get the fuck out of the car." Vinny got out;

"What are we doing here Luca? Are you going to buy a book?"

"Yeah, Head Boss for Dummies." As he said that he slapped Vinny behind the head. "I told you, I got into books when I was in the joint. I read this really good book by Giovanni Gambino and I want to see if he's got anything new out."

"Oh man really Luca, you need to stop this, you are going to be head boss. You can't be doing this shit; you have to get all this out of your mind."

"I'm going to make a lot of changes my friend, you watch and see."

They walked into the store and Vinny was looking around like this was all new to him. He was amazed how many different kinds of books there were.

"Vin, close your fucking mouth. It's like this is the first time you walked into a book store."

"It is Lu, when do I ever read a book? I'm always looking at playboy."

"Well, expand your mind; open it up and you see how much shit is out there."

They were in the fiction section looking to see if there was anything new that came out. Luca turned around and that's when he saw her. She looked confused and was looking at every title, and talking to herself. Vinny was looking at all the books too and couldn't believe how many gangster books were out.

"Vin, I'm in love."

"What the fuck are you talking about Luca?"

"There she is; my future wife, the mother of my children."

"Holy shit Luca; she's way out of your league."

Luca turned around and slapped him in the head again. "You forgot who you're talking to? Look at me; she would be privileged to be by my side. Look at those legs; they go on forever, and that long brown hair, Oh god how I would pull the shit out of that hair."

"Luca, relax yourself, I know you just got out but we are in a public place."

"Watch the master at work."

"Luca don't do this."

Luca turned to Vinny, "watch and learn."

* * * * *

NIKKI WAS TALKING TO herself, she was so confused. "Oh dear lord, there's got to be a million gangster books here. If I only knew the author it would make my life easier. I don't want to ask, I know I will find it." She knelt down and started to look at the bottom. She noticed a pair of D&G men's shoes standing next her. She thought, *nice taste, he must be gay*.

"Here, this is an amazing book, you should read it." Before she looked up she noticed he was holding the book that she was looking for; Mulberry to Rome by Giovanni Gambino.

"That's it!"

He helped her up. She still didn't look at the man that handed her the book.

"That's it how did you know I was looking for this? Was I talking to myself out loud?"

"No, it's just a really good book, if you're into gangsters."

Nikki laughed and looked up. She couldn't believe her eyes, it was Luca. She took a step back.

Luca looked at her confused, "Are you ok?"

"Yes, I'm fine. Why do you say that?"

"Because you look like you just saw a ghost."

"No, it was the sudden rush from getting up, I got a little dizzy."

"Wow, you have amazing eyes. I didn't see them when you were kneeling down."

"Ok, that is an old pick up line, get with the times."

He laughed, "You're funny."

"You think so? You don't even know me."

"Well, you are looking for this book, so you must have a sense humor."

"You read this book?"

"Yes I did and I'll let you in a little secret"; he leaned closer to her and whispered in her in ear, "They are making a movie out of it."

"And this is a big secret why?"

"Because I heard they have the most amazing lead actor."

"Oh really and who's that?" Nikki knew exactly who it was because she had heard the whole conversation.

"I can't tell you because if I did then I would have to kill you." She didn't laugh at all. "I'm kidding, it was a joke."

"Yeah I got that, thanks. So what's this book about?"

"It's really funny. It's about three gangsters who go back in time to the Roman era. It's really hysterical, you have to read it."

"That's the plan, that's why I'm getting it. Wait, how do they go back in time?"

"They have a time machine."

Nikki smiled; "I wish I had one of those." Luca just admired her smile, "Don't we all."

They were just looking into each other's eyes, when she realized what she was doing. She looked away, "Thanks again for the book."

"Wait, that's it? You're leaving?"

"Yes, I'm going to pay for the book and go."

"Listen, let me buy you the book. It will be my gift to you"

"Why? What do you want?"

"I want you to read it and call me when you're done." Luca pulled out a card with his information. Nikki took it and read it out loud; "Luca Marchisio, import and export business." She laughed, *how original.*

"What's so funny, you don't like my card?"

"No I was just thinking out loud."

"I didn't get your name."

Oh shit, she thought to herself, what the fuck was her name? She couldn't give him her real name. She looked around really quick and said the first woman name she could find on any book, she spotted one; *Bianca Monteleone.*

"Bianca, my name is Bianca."

"That's a beautiful name, Bianca you have a last name?"

"Monteleone, Bianca Monteleone."

"Oh you are Italian?"

"Yes of course, isn't everybody?"

He laughed, "I like you, you are really funny. Come on Bianca, let's check out this book. The faster you read it the faster you can call me and tell me what you think."

"Really you don't have to buy me the book."

"I know I don't but I want to, that way when you are reading it, you can think of me."

She laughed; "You are a very confident man, aren't you?"

"Why shouldn't I be, have you checked me out? I'm a good looking guy. Now walk with me and let's get you reading."

She couldn't believe this was happening. She kept thinking to herself, *what am I supposed to do now? He's my subject; I can't be hanging out with him or calling him.* She found herself drawn to him. He was a very good looking guy and he smelled so good. If she kept shaking her head like that, the thought would actually jump out of her head, she figured.

Luca turned around and looked at her, "Are you ok?"

"Yes, I'm fine. I'm just in a rush and running late."

"Running late for what, a lunch date?"

"No, work."

"What do you do?"

"What's with all the questions, you writing a book?"

"Maybe one day I will."

He paid for the book and handed it to her and walked her out. At this point Vinny was standing next to him, "Luca we got to go, I just got a call."

"Ok Vin relax, you're ruining my mojo here."

She laughed; "Oh is that what you call it?"

"Babe, listen." She did a double take, "Babe?"

"Yeah, I call everyone Babe, is that a problem?"

"Yes, you don't know me well enough to call me babe."

"Ok I'm sorry, Bianca, you have my card call me."

"Sure no problem, after I read the book."

"Are you a fast reader?"

"Yes I am, why?"

"That way I know you will be calling me in a few days." She started to walk to her car, then turned around and yelled out, "Thanks again for the book."

"The pleasure was all mine." He grabbed Vinny by the chest, "Vin, I want her."

"Ok, and I'm sure she has a man Luca. A woman like that is not single."

"I don't care what I have to do, I want her."

Nikki couldn't wait to get back to the station. She had to call Larry to tell him that something was up. She knew the look in Vinny's eyes when he told Luca he got a call. Nikki rang Larry; "Larry, where are you?"

"I'm actually heading to Luca's place now."

"Ok good, that's exactly where I want you. Move it ok, I'll be there in about fifteen minutes."

"Nikki is everything Ok?"

"Yeah I think the operation just took a turn and things are going to be different. I'll fill you in when I get there."

Nikki hung up and headed straight to Luca's apartment. As she was driving, she couldn't help but think of him. She actually enjoyed talking to him. The fact that he was easy on the eyes did help, but there was something about him that really pulled her in but she couldn't put her finger on it. "What am I suppose to do now? He seen my face, I have to figure out a way to make this work out to my advantage. I'm not playing with a little gangster; I'm going to be dealing with the big boss himself. Maybe I should call him, get in from the inside. I'll get more information. Oh dear lord he's got me talking to myself now. But he did smell good and those eyes, there's something in those eyes that just made me tingle all over. STOP!! Get this man out of your head and stop fucking talking to yourself, people are going to think you're crazy." She laughed at herself as she was pulling up next to the van. She got out and grabbed the book. She couldn't help looking at the book and smiling. She knocked on the van and George let her in.

"Look who decided to show up for work."

"George, I'm your boss, I come in and out as I please."

George rolled his eyes, 'Yeah, yeah that's what they all say."

"Hey Larry are they back yet?"

"No, not yet Nikki, what's that in your hands?"

"The book that they were talking about, I think there might be something in here that will help us figure out some shit."

"Nikki, you said that there was a change, what's up?"

"Larry, I really need to speak to the chief about it but when I was in the book store going nuts looking for this, guess who was standing right over me with this book in his hands?" Larry's face looked a little confused, "who?"

With a big grin on her face she replied, "LUCA"!

George threw his hands up in the air, "that's it we're done, close up shop. Let's go home." Nikki shot him a look, "sit your ass down and listen."

George looked at Nikki with those beady little eyes, "I love when you get all nasty, you are so hot!"

"George if you don't want me to shoot you I suggest you sit your ass down and shut your stupid mouth."

She turned to Larry and started to explain to him what will happen now.

"Listen to this, I work from the inside. He gave me his card, he told me after I finish the book to give him a call so we can go and discuss it. So at first I thought, NO WAY, this is crazy and it will ruin the whole operation but then driving here I decided that it would be a great idea because I can get in. I can hear and see more."

"Nikki, you know that the chief will not go for that, we are not dealing with little people here, we are dealing with the mob."

"Larry why wouldn't he go for it, because I'm a woman and he thinks I can't handle myself. Well, I'll have you know that I box every morning and I can take out the whole fucking team."

George rolls his eyes, "Yeah ok how about you and me go one on one?"

"I played that game before with you George and you suck!"

Larry laughed, "Oh man that was LOW"!

George feeling all beat up looked at Larry, "shut up asshole."

"Ok boys enough, I'm not here to baby-sit you two. So Larry what do you think?"

"I don't know Nikki, it's dangerous. What do you think your husband will say?"

"I'm not worried about Brian right now, he knows this is my job and he has to deal with it."

George decided to put his two cents in; "Nikki you have a grin on your face if I didn't know any better, I say you are starting to like this gangster."

"Of course I am. He's going to help me bring them all down."

Larry interrupted the two of them, "Hey guys, they are here."

"OK, let's listen and see what the call was about."

Both men looked at her Nikki, "what call?"

"Shhhh, I want to hear everything."

CHAPTER 5

LUCA COULDN'T STOP THINKING of Bianca. She was gorgeous. She was an angel sent from heaven. She looked so smart and she seemed like a tough cookie, he really liked that in a woman. He had to shake her out of his head; there was a chance that she wouldn't call. He thought for a second, *yeah ok I'm too hot, she'll call.* But he needed a distraction for now.

"Vin, who was on the phone?"

"It was Matteo; he said the boss had a job for us."

"Really, already? I just got out. I figured I'd start after this weekend."

"Yeah well Luca, we don't take vacations unless we are six feet under or in the joint. Even when we are away we are always working."

Luca looked at his friend, "Ain't that the fucking truth? Where are we meeting them Vin?"

"Your place."

"Great let's go." Luca and Vinny parked the car and went up to Luca's apartment. Luca just threw himself on the couch, "Man what a day"

"I know and it's only three in the afternoon."

"Vin, what time are the boys coming by?"

"He said in a half hour, so they should be here soon."

"Vin, I can't get that beauty out of my head."

"I'm sure she got you out of her head."

"Oh no Vin, she's thinking of me right now. She's wondering what I'm doing. She's going to call, I can bet on it."

"Hey Luca, why don't you ask her to come to the party this weekend?"

"That's a great idea but I don't have her number, I have to wait for her to call me."

"I thought you just said you were sure she was going to call?" Luca grabbed the pillow next him and threw it at Vinny's head. "Smart ass"!! Vinny was about to throw it back when they heard a knock at the door. Luca jumped up and went to open the door.

"Matteo, Andrea, boys how the heck are you?"

"Luca my man, how the hell have you been?" Matteo gave Luca a big hug.

"Under the circumstances not bad at all."

"Luca, it's great to see you," Andrea gave Luca a big hug.

"Andrea what's up with the gut, you putting on some weight there?"

"Yeah I know Luca; marriage will do that to you."

'That's right, you got married, Congrats my man. How's the married life?

Andrea rubbed his belly, "what do you think Luca?" They all laughed; Luca pointed to the couch,

"Sit down boys, what do you have for us? What does the boss want?"

Matteo looked at Luca, "Remember about ten years ago, Philip D took care of that guy, Nicky "big feet" Bonello?"

"Oh yeah, something about him sleeping with his girl or something"

"Yeah that one, anyway, this jerk off has been talking in his sleep for the last ten fucking years about where he buried the guy. The guy got pinched and his wife his concerned that the security guard are going to hear him talk in his sleep."

Luca looked at Matteo confused, "Ok Matteo where we going with this?"

Andrea with a big sigh said,

"The boss wants to move the body so if they do hear him, the body will be gone."

Luca looked at Vinny, "Are you serious about this? I have to go remove a body that's been fucking buried for ten fucking years? It's bones for god sakes!" Matteo got up,

"Luca listen nowadays they can find out who a person is with a strand of hair."

Luca agreed, "Ok so when are we supposed to do this?"

Matteo and Andrea looked at each other and they both answered, "Tonight!"

"Ok, so you guys coming too?"

"No we can't, we have a party."

Luca looked at all of them, "Are you fucking kidding me? When did that ever stop us from working? What the fuck, you guys are just scared shit to dig up a dead body"!

"Luca, come on", Andrea looking at him like what he was saying was true.

"It's ok I've been off for four years, Vin and I will take care of it."

The boys got ready to leave, and Matteo turned around and asked, "So Luca you going to be at this party this weekend, right'?

"Yeah of course, it's in my honor you dumb fuck why wouldn't I go?"

Matteo laughed, "You never change you sarcastic fuck."

"Hey watch that mouth, you kiss your kids with that mouth?"

Andrea stopped and asked Luca, "Who you bringing, anyone good?"

Luca turned and looked at Vin, who just grinned.

"I met this woman, I was thinking of asking her."

Matteo laughed, "one day out of the fucking joint and you already hooking up, you never change my friend."

Luca smacked Matteo on the head, "ok, I went in the joint, I didn't fucking die!"

"Alright Luca, take care ok. Be careful tonight and I'll see you Sunday."

"Alright boys, enjoy your party tonight."

Vinny started to laugh, "yeah have a piece a cake for us, seeing that we couldn't get the day off for it."

* * * * *

Larry LOOKED AT NIKKI, "Are you the woman he's talking about?"

Nikki blushed, "I think so."

George smiled, "yeah, that's going to go over very well with the chief."

"Shut up George, when I want your opinion I'll ask you for it." Nikki started to summarize the conversation out loud, "Ok so they are going to dig up the body of Nicky Bonello, and now we know who took care of him. This is all good but we need more, this case is been dead for ten years."

Larry looked at her. "Nikki, but it's still good."

"Oh I know Larry but Philip D is a nobody, and I want the big boys."

"So are you going to call him?"

"I don't know George it might actually be a good idea if I did. I could go to the party, all the big heads will be there."

"Nikki I still think it's too dangerous."

"Larry please, I'm a big girl."

"Yeah and they have big guns!"

"So do I Larry."

"Ok well before you do anything you have to get clearance from the chief."

"George has a point Nikki."

"I know, and I'm actually a little nervous to tell him. Ok let's stop talking about and let's go talk to the chief."

They wrapped up and they all left to meet at the headquarters. Nikki was already there when George and Larry walked in. George looked at Nikki, "What the fuck, who are you Mario Andretti? How the fuck did you get here before us?"

"I know how to drive."

"Did you go in to see the chief yet?"

"No Larry, I was waiting for you guys. What did you do, hit every red light?"

George rolled his eyes, "No Mario we drove like normal people."

"Aren't you funny, ok come on boys, let's go in and talk to the chief."

Nikki knocked on the door.

"Come in guys." Chief looks up from the paper work on his desk, "to what do I owe this pleasure? I got the whole team in here. Something is up if you are all in here. Sit down, tell me what you want." The boys sat down but Nikki remained standing.

"Chief today was a little different."

"What do you mean Nikki?"

"Well, I went to the book store to get something and I ran into Luca Marchisio."

"You came face to face with your subject?"

"Yes, but I didn't mean to."

"Ok, so what happened?"

"Well, he tried picking me up."

"That's just great Nikki; he knows your face now."

"Listen, Chief I have an idea; he wants me to call him."

'WHAT?"

"Just hear me out for a minute, humor me."

"I'm listening, but I'm losing my patience Nikki."

"He wants me to call him, to tell him how the book is. We were listening today, they were ordered to go dig up the body of Nicky Bonello. We know where it is and they are moving it tonight."

"Ok this is good development."

"This weekend they are having a big welcome back party for Luca and when we were listening he said he wanted to ask me to go. Chief this is good, I can go in from the inside. Him seeing me can work to our advantage."

"Nikki, I see where you are going with this but it's too dangerous."

Larry finally spoke, "I told you." Nikki shot a look at Larry, "SHUT UP!"

"Why Chief? Because I'm a woman? Come on this case is my baby."

"Nikki this will involve more men on the case, more money."

"Why Chief?"

"Well for one we can't have you living at home, we are talking about the mob. They will follow you; they can't know who you are. So we have to set you up in an apartment. You can't put Brian at risk. Did you really think this through?"

"Chief, they are making him boss, don't you think it will all be worth it when we take them all down? Look at the big picture."

"Nikki you are making it hard for me to say no."

"Well that's the point."

The Chief looked at all three of them, "Ok but Nikki the first sign of danger I'm pulling you out."

"Yes, sure whatever you say."

"We have apartments we can set you up in."

"Chief no offence, but the mob isn't stupid. They know our so called apartments. I will find a place. And another thing, if I'm going to be playing his girlfriend, the bugs in the apartment have to come out. I'll be there and I don't need any more attention on me."

George stood up, "are you going to sleep with him? I knew you liked him."

The chief looked at George, "is that the only thing in your head? She wants the bugs out because if she's going to be hanging out there and he finds a bug he will think she planted it there, putting her in danger."

Nikki looked at the chief, "thank you at least someone in this room has brains."

"Nikki, do what you have to but please be careful. Let me know about the party, we need to set you up with wires."

"With all due respect chief but ARE YOU NUTS! You know they are going to be checking everyone that walks in, you want me to be an open target?"

"Ok, you're right. You guys still in here? Get to work!"

Nikki walked out with a huge grin on her face.

Larry patted her on the back, "Good job Nikki."

"I know Larry, I'm so excited."

George standing next to her asked, "What are you more excited about? That you got permission to date him or that you will bust them?"

Nikki slapped him upside the head, "George go to the van, we have a body to go dig up." She walked over to her desk and started to look at her messages when she turned and saw the same two goons from the other night, now they were in the office with Mike and the Chief. *How big is this bust? What is going on here?* Mike noticed Nikki looking into the office and he walked over and closed the blinds so she couldn't see anything. "What the fuck was that all about? I do not like this one bit." She jumped when her cell phone rang, it was Brian. She suddenly got a sick feeling in her stomach because now she had to explain to him that she would have to move out until the case was over.

Nikki cleared her throat, "Hey honey, what's up?"

Brian on the other end sounding a little upset, "nothing honey, I was just thinking of you."

"Brian are you Ok, you sound upset."

"Well, not really upset Nikki, just a little disappointed."

"What's wrong?"

"I actually have to go away for a week." Nikki was a little relieved.

"Why? Where are you going?"

"Well, they have this training that they want me to attend; they want to make me chief."

"Honey that's amazing!"

"I know but I don't want to leave you, especially now with your case and all."

"Brian you know what, it's your job and I knew this when I married you plus with this case I will be out on surveillance a lot, so we won't see each other much. So go and do what you have to."

"You see Nikki, this is why I love you."

"I love you too. When are you leaving?"

"Tonight after work, I won't be home to say goodbye? So please Nikki be careful."

"I will and you too."

"Ok, I love you."

"I love you too."

She hung up and just stared at her cell. Why didn't she believe him? What training could he go to for fireman chief? She didn't realize George was standing next to her.

"You didn't tell him did you?"

She jumped; "You scared the shit out of me George."

"Sorry, I didn't mean to."

"It's Ok; I was just in deep thought. No, I didn't tell him. He will be away so why worry him while he's working."

George looked at her, "Ok if that's how you want to look at it."

She changed the subject,

"Have we heard anything on the boys?"

"Yeah Larry said they were at the apartment, they ordered take out and were getting ready for the midnight digging."

She smiled; "This should be an interesting night."

"Come on, Nikki; let's go get something to eat."

At first she hesitated but she agreed, "Ok I'm game."

"WOW I'm surprised, I was waiting for a "go drop dead George", or "over my dead body."

She laughed, "I'm sorry George I don't mean to be so hard on you, but you are truly an asshole and you fucked with me and when you fuck with me, you never live it down. Plus, I am kind of hungry and don't feel like eating at the desk."

George put his arm around her, "You see that's the Nikki I know and love."

"Get your arm off me before I shoot it off."

George blushed, "over board?"

Nikki responded without looking at him and heading towards the door, "yeah just a little."

CHAPTER 6

"LUCA, WHAT'S WRONG? WHAT are you thinking about?"

"Nothing Vin, just staring into space."

"Lu, I know you too well to know you are heavy in thought."

"Vin, really, what if I wrote a book about my time in the joint?"

"Lu, you really need to get this out of your head. I really fear for your life."

"Vin, I think Mr. B. would be fine with it. It's not like I'm ratting anyone out. And the movie is fiction it's not naming anyone. For god sakes it's got a time machine. How the fuck is that going to affect the family?"

"That's not what it's about, you are going to be boss, and you will have the press and all those paparazzi's all over you. How are we supposed to do what we do if we have cameras all over us?"

"Yeah, but Vin think about it. It will distract them from the family. They will be following me waiting for me to do something, while the family does what they have to do."

"Ok let's not talk about this now; we have a body to dig up."

"I have to change."

"Why?"

"Vin, do you actually think I'm going to dig up a body in my Dolce & Gabbana shoes?"

"Ok well hurry up, the faster we go, the faster we finish."

"Vin, are you scared?"

"No, but come on Luca, it's a dead man."

"Vin, he's all fucking bones!" Luca slapped him on the head, "come one Vin, you got a little soft"

"No I didn't."

"Whatever, I'm going to change."

"Ok, I'm making an espresso, you want one?"

"Yeah nice and strong, don't make it like dirty fucking water. I had enough of that shit for four years."

Vinny was flipping through the channels on the TV getting all restless waiting for Luca. "Lu, come on already."

Luca came out stood in front of Vinny, "how does this look?" Luca was wearing a black Fila jump suit.

"Gorgeous Luca, like the dead guy is going to give a fuck what you're wearing."

"OH you never know who you could run into in the middle of the night."

Vinny rolled his eyes, "In that case go put on your D&G shoes on again."

"Nah, they won't go with this."

Vinny started laughing, "You're too much my friend."

When they got to the site and no one was around.

"Luca it's creepy out here."

"Vin you really are starting to annoy me. The faster we do this, the faster I go home and get to bed. Vin do we have a map or are we digging up the whole freaking junk yard? Please tell me you have an idea where he is."

"Yeah, he should be around here."

"Great that's really helpful. Well come on Vin let's start. You got the shovel?"

"I thought you got it. Oh man Vin I'm losing my patience here."

"I'm kidding Luca, relax."

"Ok that's not funny."

The boys looked at each other and grabbed a shovel. It was dark and past midnight. Luca had his mind on Bianca.

"Yo Vin what did you think of that *'bella Cavadda'* we saw today at the book store?"

"WHAT?"

"Vin, I'm starting to think that since I've been away you lost every bit of knowledge I ever taught you. "Who the fuck were you hanging out with when I was away?"

"Nobody, just the guys."

"Ok so you don't know what I just said? When we see a beautiful girl and she has that walk, that long mane of hair, what do we call them when they walk in?"

"I got it Luca."

"Vin, what's wrong with you?"

"Nothing Luca, I'm just tired and this is making me sick. The smell is getting to me."

"OK let's hurry up."

"But Luca I think she is beautiful. I don't know about her calling you."

"Vin, you see I have a shovel in my hands right? You are talking to the man, she will call."

"Ok let's see."

As they were just about to finish up Vinny's phone rang; he had a really loud annoying ring tone.

Luca jumped, "OH WHAT THE FUCK IS THAT?"

Oh that's my ring tone."

"Vin really, can't you change that?"

"I like it."

"Then put it on vibrate when you are with me. It's annoying."

"It's the boys they want to know if we are done."

"Yeah just tell them we are wrapping up."

CHAPTER 7

NIKKI ARRIVED HOME TO AN empty apartment. Brian had left for the training. She was a little happy about that. She didn't want to explain today's events because she knew Brian wouldn't like it. She made herself a cup of coffee and decided to start reading the book. She wanted to hurry up and finish it. Did she want to finish it so she could call Luca back, or did she want to know what was hidden in the book? She was very determined and either way she was going find out what was going on. She found herself laughing as she was reading. "Oh my God this is really funny." So far no clues. Being a great detective she did read very fast. She needed to call Luca so he could invite her to the party this weekend. That gave her six days. She fell asleep reading and the alarm woke her up. She jumped up out of bed. "Oh shit I want to hit the gym before I start my day." She got up and the book fell off her lap. She remembered she was reading, looked at the book and laughed; "what a funny book." She was going to finish it today and call Luca. She took a quick shower and ran out of the apartment. She would be back for her stuff later. She was going to a new apartment today. She had to play her new role as Bianca Monteleone. She was actually very excited about it. She got to the gym and put on her boxing gloves. Nikki loved to box. She was very fit and didn't miss a morning of working out. She couldn't start her day without it. She finished her work out, took a quick shower and went to the office to check in. She spoke to Larry to see how it went last night and he said they moved the body and knew exactly where they put it.

"I have the report but keeping it in the file until the very end."

"Of course Larry thanks."

"Nikki where are you?"

"I'm at the office I want to finish this book; I have a few chapters left. I was up all night reading it."

"How is it?"

"Larry it's hysterical, now I know how we got Caesar Salad."

"What?"

"Nothing you can read it after I'm done, but I'll tell you one thing, there are no hidden clues in here."

"So you read it for nothing?"

"Oh no it was actually really good, I have a few more chapters. Why don't you and George stay on top of Luca today? I will touch base with you later."

"Sure, he's still sleeping but I will call you if anything interesting comes up."

"Thanks Larry."

"Oh, Nikki, did you find a place?"

"I'm working on it, but it has to be today."

Nikki hung up with Larry and picked up the book so she could finish it. She was eager and wanted to call Luca today. She wanted him to invite her to the big bash this weekend. So that meant, calling him today, hopefully a date and then he could ask her. She was really into the book when she got distracted by those two goons again. *What the hell is Mike working on?* Just as she was going to approach them the chief called her in the office.

"What's up chief?"

"Are you all set in your new place yet?"

"No, I haven't found anything yet"

"Well, I found something midtown, maybe you can go take a look at it?"

"Sure no problem, what's the address"

"I already saw it and I actually told the agent you will be taking it, it's really the best place and as far as our budget goes, it works. It's 1010 Williams Street"

"Oh ok, I know exactly where that is, I'll go and take a look now."

The chief gave her the name and number of the agent. Nikki made the call and left the office right away. Mike watched her leave and looked at the chief by the corner of his eye with approval. Nikki wasn't dumb she knew they were trying to get her out of the office. She noticed Mike the whole time and the look that he gave the chief. *They are up to something and I'm going to find out what it is.* It was a really nice day and she decided she was going to put the top down on her mustang. She loved the wind blowing in her hair. As she arrived at the apartment, she scoped out her surroundings. It's what she did she was a fed and always watching her back. She noticed a Starbucks on the corner and thought to herself, *now that I like, to have my mocha nearby always is a plus.* She met the agent outside the apartment, she looked nervous and in a rush.

"Hi, Marie?"

"Yes, Bianca Monteleone?"

"That's me in the flesh"

"I pictured you a lot shorter, wow to have some of your height would be great."

They laughed and Marie led Nikki upstairs to apartment 214L. The area was really nice. Everything was nearby and it was busy. Nikki liked that hustle and bustle so she felt she would fit right in. *I don't mind the noise either, hell I'm noisy myself.* The agent opened the door and Nikki fell in love. The apartment was pretty much a big open space. It had two columns in the middle of the room and huge window with the view of the Brooklyn Bridge. It was painted all white and it looked very clean. Overall it was about 2000 square feet of living and she definitely felt she could get used to that. It looked brand new and the bathroom was spotless and very European. It was already furnished which would save her plenty of time. The bedroom was amazing. It had a nice canopy bed in the middle of the room with an amazing view and a little veranda to go and sit outside on those beautiful cool brisk nights. *I definitely love this place.* Nikki knew the department had to be paying a pretty penny for this but she didn't care.

"So tell me Marie, can I move in today?"

"Yes of course, your dad had said you were desperate and this is our newest and available suite now."

"That's great, got to love my dad for taking the time out of his busy schedule to place his only daughter in a place like this."

"Yes, he was here earlier today checking it out; he even gave me a deposit for it. So you can move in right now."

"Did he?"

Nikki had a bad taste in her mouth; she didn't like this at all. Why was the chief so concerned that he came himself to put a deposit on this? Something didn't seem right, but she was going to get to the bottom of it.

"Thank you Marie for coming back to show it to me, did you happen to give my dad an extra set of keys?"

"Yes, he requested them and really Bianca it's no bother at all. Here is my card, if you need anything at all, please don't hesitate to call."

"Thank you so much."

The agent handed Nikki the keys and left. Nikki decided to scope out the place and look for bugs. She had a special gadget that would see if they were any bugs. She walked around and lo and behold she found a few. She removed every one of them. "I specifically said NO BUGS!" She was pissed and stormed out. She headed back to the office and walked right into the office. Mike was in there with the chief.

"What crawled up your ass?"

"Get out Mike; I need to talk to MY DAD!"

"Chief, I didn't know she was your daughter." Mike laughed and walked out staring right into Nikki's eyes.

"I'm watching you Mike"

"Oh I watch you all the time Nikki, you are so hot how can I not?"

"ASSHOLE!"

"I love you too Nikki."

Mike and Nikki didn't get along very well. Mike was always stealing her cases and rubbing his victories in her face. When the chief made Nikki the head of this operation, Mike was pissed. He always got the good cases, so he was going out of his way to make sure Nikki would fall flat on her face. Nikki slammed the door.

"Chief what is going on?"

"What are you talking about?"

"What's with all the bugs in my new place?"

"Nikki it's procedure."

"Yes and I said NO BUGS, don't you trust me to report back?"

"It's not you I don't trust. I just want to make sure you are safe."

"I appreciate that but I'm a grown woman and I can handle a little gangster, as you may have heard, I ripped all the bugs out."

"Yes, I heard. Nikki you need to be careful."

"Another thing chief."

"What?"

"What is Mike working on? I'm getting really tired of those goons staring at me when I walk in."

"Nothing, just a little drug case we are working on."

She just stared at him for a few minutes and then walked out of the office. She was going to find out, but right now she had a gangster to call. She had bigger fish to fry and this little thing with Mike will have to wait.

CHAPTER 8

LUCA WAS JUST GETTING out of bed. He had a long night with Vinny. He was going over the events of the night with his buddy and couldn't help but laugh. He kept thinking how Vinny was scared to touch the dead body. He started to make his espresso when his phone rang.

"Talk to me."

"Luca?"

Luca realized that it wasn't Vinny or one of his boys. This person had an angelic voice and her tone lingered through his whole body.

"Yeah, who's this?"

"It's Bianca Monteleone."

Luca just froze and fixed himself as if she could see him.

"Hey Babe, what's up?"

"BABE?"

"Oh that's right, I haven't earned the right to call you that yet, I'm sorry. How are you BIANCA?"

"You are one SMART ASS you know that?"

"Yeah I've been called worse things but that's Ok. Don't tell me you finished the book already?"

"Yes, I did. I told you I was a fast reader."

"I don't believe you. You called me because you missed me and dying to see me."

"Don't flatter yourself Luca."

"So what did you think of the book?"

"It was really funny, I liked it a lot."

"See, you stick with me and I will you lead in all the right directions."

"Yes that's the plan."

"So Bianca, how about we hook up tonight, say dinner?"

"I don't know Luca, I really don't know you that well."

"But you called."

"Yes because I made a promise, and I always keep my promises."

"That's a good thing to know. Let me take you out to dinner, I promise you can trust me and I too keep my promises."

"Ok fine, I guess I can meet you."

"What time should I pick you up?"

"Around seven is fine."

"How about you give me your number and your address?"

Bianca gave him all the information. They said their goodbyes and hung up.

Luca looked at the phone, "She wants me." He didn't even put it down, he had to call Vinny and rub it in his face.

"Vin, wake up and get your ass here."

"Luca, it's so early, please let me sleep a little more."

"You can sleep when you're dead."

Vinny woke up and jumped out of bed;

"Luca what are you saying? Do you know something? Are they getting rid of me?"

Luca couldn't help but laugh, "You are such an asshole, like I would make them touch you. It's an expression Vin, now get your ass down here before I kill you."

"Ok, Ok, I'm up, I'll be there in the few minutes."

* * * * *

NIKKI LOOKED AT HER phone and wondered what she was getting herself into. She was a little nervous about meeting Luca, but not because he was a gangster, but because she was attracted to him. She never felt this attraction with any of her subjects. She was in deep thought when her phone rang. She jumped because she was looking at it.

"Hello."

"Bianca?"

"Yes"

"Ok, making sure you gave me the right number."

"Luca?"

"Yeah, it's me."

"What do you think I am fifteen, and giving you fake numbers?"

"I wanted to make sure that's all"

"Well it's me."

"All right then I'll see you tonight at seven."

She was all smiles when she hung up. She thought *oh my god I feel fifteen.* The phone rang again but this time it was Larry.

"Nikki, I heard you have a hot date tonight."

"That's right I forgot you guys are listening."

"Nikki you do know we are following you tonight?"

"Of course, I wouldn't have it any other way, once I find out where we are going I'll give you the address."

Nikki had to go to her apartment and pack her clothes. She wasn't sure where Luca was taking her and she was a little nervous. She never interacted with her subjects, it just wasn't allowed. This wasn't a date in her eyes. It was work but for some reason she was very excited and felt like a school girl who was going out with the popular guy in school. She got home and remembered that Brian wasn't around. She did have to tell him eventually that the operation has changed. She knew he would be upset and very worried. She started to pack her belongings so she could go to the new apartment. She collected all her stuff and walked out.

* * * * *

LUCA WAS STARTING TO get ready for his big date. He couldn't decide on what to wear. It had been four years since he'd been away so he wasn't sure on what to wear, or what was in. He sent Vinny to D&G to pick up a few things. Just as he was about to call him, Vinny knocked on the door.

"Well it's about fucking time. Did you make the clothes yourself?"

"Lu, knowing how particular you are, I couldn't decide on what to get."

"Ok, I forgive you, just this one time. So let's see what you got."

Vinny showed Luca the black Dolce & Gabbana suit he had picked up along with an amazing blue shirt to go with it.

"I was going to pick up some ties, but I know you are not a fan of ties."

"And you are so right my friend, you know me too well. This suit is Sharp. Vin, I take back any insulting thing I've said to you since I got out."

"Oh good, I'm glad I redeemed myself. Luca, you really like this one huh?"

"Vin, I don't know what she did to me in that book store but when those big green eyes looked at mine, I felt like lightning struck."

"You mean like cupid hit you with an arrow?"

"No! fuck cupid and his arrow, he can stick that arrow where the sun don't shine. Vin, this was different, she hit me like a lightning bolt, and she went right through me. I'm telling you Vin, I think I finally met my match."

"And you got all this with one look?"

"Sometimes that's all you need. The attraction, the beauty and her smart ass mouth, why she's a female version of me, how can I not love her?"

"Lu, you talked for ten minutes and you are talking about love. I honestly think you got really fucked up in that joint. Ok let me ask you a question, if you were on a cliff and on one hand you had Bianca and the other hand your mother and you had to let go of one who would you choose?"

"YOU! you fucking idiot for asking me the stupid question!"

Luca went inside to get changed and continued his conversation from the bathroom.

"Vin, is The Cave still opened?"

"Yeah, that place is amazing and the business is great, they are never closing."

"Do I need reservations?"

"No, it's a hole in the wall but the best fucking one out there. Is that where you are taking her?"

"No, I just felt like talking about it, of course that's where I want to go. They have the best sushi and the most romantic setting. She is going to be putty in my hands tonight."

"I don't know Luca she seems tough, you might have a little challenge on your hands."

Luca came out of the bathroom and spun around for Vinny.

"What do you think my man?"

"I think I picked the right suit for you, you look sharp."

"Yeah I know, and you know me, I'm always up for a good challenge."

Luca got his stuff together, put on some D&G cologne and was ready to head out.

"Oh, give me your keys to the Maserati."

"NO WAY! I love that car too much and I know how you drive."

"Vin, I look this hot, there's no way I'm driving your other shit box of a car, come on hand them over."

"Oh come on Luca, you are going to give me a heart attack. That car is my baby."

"Don't worry, uncle Luca will take good care of it. Now hand them over and stop acting like a little girl."

Vinny took out the keys and handed them over to Luca. He fought on letting them go and Luca slapped him in the head.

"Let GO!"

"Luca I swear if something happens to that car, you will have me to deal with."

"Vin, look at me shaking, I'm so scared."

Luca walked out and Vinny ran after him, "I mean it Luca. Oh, I'm talking to you! FINE! HAVE FUN!"

Luca got in the car and admired the Italian beauty for a few minutes. He wrapped his hands around the wheel and took a deep breath. "I love this car, maybe a little more than women." He paused, thinking, *YEAH, OK NEVER.* He started the car and ripped out smoking the tires while poor Vinny came out the window screaming, "I HATE YOU!" George and Larry were on his tail. They didn't stay too close as they knew where he was going anyway.

*   *   *   *   *

NIKKI WAS GETTING READY and was undecided on what she should wear. Should she get all sexy, or should she just go casual and comfortable? *Why am I having a hard time with this? It's just work.* She tried to convince herself that she was not attracted to Luca but couldn't help but smile on the thought that he called her back to see if she gave him the right number. She decided to wear her black leggings, with her blue long, sexy, but sophisticated, Dolce & Gabbana top. The top was a little low cut but long enough that it came mid-thigh. She decided to finish the look with her favourite D&G boots with three inch heels. She was already tall, and the heels put her over six feet. She didn't wear a lot of make up so she decided to stay her natural self, just enough to bring out her eyes. Just as she was finishing up the door bell rang. She turned and looked at the door and she got a very nervous feeling. Her stomach was in knots and felt like butterflies. Looking at herself one last time she grabbed her purse and headed for the door. She opened the door and Luca was amazed. "WOW, you look amazing." Nikki blushed and felt the heat on her face.

"Thank you, you don't look so bad yourself."

"Aren't you going to invite me in?"

"No, not at all."

"Why not?"

Nikki put her hand on his chest as she pushed him out, "No BABE you have to earn that right."

Luca's mouth dropped,

"Babe, that's my word."

"I'm sorry I don't recall you earning that right either."

"Wait, you can call me babe but I can't."

"That's right BABE."

She locked the door and walked in front of him. Luca just stared at her and bit his lower lip

"Che Cavadda!"

"I'm sorry what did you just call me?"

"Nothing, I was talking to myself"

"Did you just call me a horse?"

"You know Italian?"

"Doesn't everyone? Why did you call me a horse? That's not nice."

"It's a compliment; it's a beauty like you. You have the long legs and the long hair, you are amazing, and you know, a Philly?"

"That's weird I never heard of that expression."

"It's a man thing, you would call a man a Stallion we call the beautiful women *'Cavadda'*."

"Yeah, Ok whatever, where are we going?"

"You are one tough *Cavadda*"

"OK you call me that one more time and I go back upstairs."

"Ok, I'm sorry."

CHAPTER 9

LUCA COULDN'T TAKE HIS eyes off Nikki. He was amazed how beautiful she was and the way the moonlight hit her golden brown long hair, he felt like he died and went to heaven. He was a true gentleman. He opened the door for her to get into the car. She was very impressed. She smiled and thanked him. He got into the driver's seat and just sat there, looking at her.

"What, do I have something hanging out of my nose?"

He couldn't help but laugh. "No. You are so funny. I do have to say this Bianca and believe me when I tell you it's not a line, you have the most captivating smile, it lights up a whole room."

Nikki realized for the first time tonight that her name was Bianca. She couldn't help but blush. She actually felt his sincerity when he said that to her.

"Thank you Luca, that's really sweet of you."

"Oh and another thing, I didn't want to say it before because then I would have to sit and wait for you to change, but we match tonight."

Nikki looked at him and then looked at herself. Before she had a chance to say let me go back upstairs to change, Luca started the engine and took off.

"Oh man Luca, this is so corny. Please let me go back and change."

"No, you look HOT and I want to show you off tonight. If you haven't realized it, you are wearing my favorite designer."

"Yes, I noticed the D&G suit, just like I noticed the shoes at the book store."

"A woman who finally knows what Style really is."

"And a man who doesn't need a woman to dress him, I have to say Luca, I'm very impressed."

"Oh, it's me Luca Marchisio; I have a reputation to uphold."

Nikki couldn't help but laugh. She just looked at Luca and couldn't take her eyes off him. She thought to herself, *he really isn't that bad.* He looked very handsome and he did have the most amazing eyes. There was something about them when he looked at her that made her feel like a school girl. For the first time tonight she actually considered this a date and not work. She had to stop and get that out of her head. In reality, he was a gangster and she was here to bust him and the whole mob. She couldn't get emotionally involved. She had to shake the thought out of her.

"So where are we going?"

"You ever heard of the Cave?"

"The Cave, what is the Cave?"

"Oh my God, I can't believe you never went to the Cave."

"Now you are making me nervous. Where the heck is this Cave? And what is it a strip joint or something?"

"I'm a little insulted that you would think I would take such a beautiful woman like you to a degrading place like that. Plus the girls would all feel intimated the minute you walk through that door because all the men would have their eyes on you."

"I have to give it to you Luca you have a way with words."

"I'm good, I know. Years of practice, the Cave is the most amazing place to have sushi."

"Oh, I have to tell you I hate sushi."

"WHAT? No, you don't hate sushi. You just haven't had sushi with me. And hate is such a strong word, have you ever tried it?"

"Yes I did once and I'm not a fan of raw fish."

"Oh babe, I mean Bianca you don't know what you're missing. It's not all raw. Just try it if you don't like it we can go somewhere else. You have to be open to trying new things."

"Ok well since you put it that way, I guess it won't kill me, RIGHT?"

Luca couldn't stop laughing she was like a little girl who was afraid of the trying the big scary roller coaster and needed confirmation that it was all going to be alright.

"You really are funny, as anyone ever told you; you should've been a comedian?"

"I guess I missed my calling."

They pulled up to The Cave, it really was a hole in the wall but there was line down block. Luca wasn't worried he knew the owners and he would have no problem at all getting in.

The parking valet guy walked over to Luca and looked at the car, "nice wheels."

Luca handed him the keys "if I see as much as a piece of hair on this car, you are a dead man'.

The boy got really nervous "no sir, I'll park it in our VIP section."

Luca handed the kid a twenty, "good boy."

Luca walked over to Bianca and put his arm around her waist.

"So what do you think?"

"I think we are eating McDonald's tonight, we are never getting in here. Do you not see this line?"

"I'm sorry are you with your typical Joe or are you with Luca Marchisio? I think you forget who you are with."

"Well technically I don't know you that well, so right now I am with your typical Joe."

"Oh you have so much to learn."

The bouncer recognized Luca and gave him a big hug and hand shake.

"Luca it's so good to see you we missed you. When did you get out?"

"A few days ago."

The bouncer looked at Nikki, "you don't waste any time my friend."

"Isn't she a beauty?"

"You're not kidding, where did you find this one?"

Nikki was getting really annoyed, "Hello, I am standing right here."

"Yeah I know, that's why we are staring at you."

"Luca, the usual room?"

"Of course my man, I wouldn't have it any other way."

The bouncer escorted them both in to a really secluded room in the back. The Cave was a very exclusive restaurant. The only lighting in the whole place was candles placed on each table. It was very dark and didn't have your typical tables and chairs, but instead it had couches and little coffee tables. The room was all the way in the back. Inside were couches with throw pillows and a curtain for privacy. Only the VIP guests got that room and tonight, Luca and Bianca were VIPs. Nikki was very impressed. She really liked the place it was a very romantic setting. She couldn't understand why she never heard of this place. Maybe the fact that she didn't eat sushi had something to do with it. Luca said hello to almost everyone in the room. He was a regular here. He handed the bouncer a fifty and thanked him. "Luca anything you want, don't hesitate to ask." Luca shook his hand, "thanks man, I appreciate it. I really missed this place." They sat down and the bouncer closed the curtains.

"What is this place?"

"Don't worry about it, no one is going to come in and give you a lap dance."

Nikki laughed, "I hope not."

"Is that a smile? You just lit up this whole place, great now it's not a cave anymore."

They both laughed and Luca just bit his lower lip. He couldn't stop looking at her. There was something about this woman that just drove him nuts. Luca wasn't one to be hit this hard by a woman before. Usually the women are falling all over him and she wasn't doing that. Maybe that was why he was so intrigued with her. She was a challenge and he rarely got a woman who challenged him.

"This really is a nice a place, too bad I don't like sushi."

"There you go again Bianca, let me show you how great sushi is."

The waitress walked in and she knew Luca. She gave him a look.

"Hey Luca how are you?"

"Good Monica, how are you?"

"Still waiting for your call, when did you get out?"

"A few days ago."

"You look great. What can I get you to drink?"

"Why don't you start us off with two Mango Martini's"

"Sure no problem."

Luca looked at Nikki to see the expression on her face.

"Did you want something else? They make the best Mango Martini here and you need to try it."

"No I'm good with that, I don't mind trying something new"

"See now you're talking."

"Luca, that's the second person who asked you when you got out, where did you get out of?"

"I was in a mental institution for four years, they let me out on good behaviour, and after I stopped biting the head doctor they thought I was good enough to go."

Nikki had to play the part and act dumb, she had to look nervous and surprised at the same time.

"WHAT?"

"I'm kidding Babe."

She shot him a look of disapproval on the "babe" calling.

"Come on, I still didn't earn the right?"

"Listen I'm not your typical bimbo and being called BABE isn't my thing. I don't know you well enough for you to call me "Babe". For all I know you could be this psycho who just got released from a, like you said, a mental institution."

"Ok I wasn't in a mental institution; I was away for a crime I didn't commit."

"Great even better, you're a mass murderer."

"No I'm not I'm actually a really nice guy who is against violence, but I hate rats and I will never be one or around one for that matter."

Nikki's eyes just went straight to the floor, she actually believed him for the first time that he didn't commit the crime that he was in for. She found him to be real sincere. Was she starting to get soft?

"So what do you actually do Luca?"

"You really don't know who I am?"

"No, I don't, am I supposed to know?"

"Listen let's just enjoy tonight and forget about me, let's talk about you what do you do?"

Nikki hadn't thought about this, what was she going to tell him? *Oh, I'm a fed and I'm here to bust you and your whole family. Yeah, that wouldn't go over too well.* She had to think fast. Her passion other than being a Fed was taking pictures. She did a lot of free lance.

"I'm actually a photographer I do a lot of free lance work."

"Really that's amazing, you should take a lot of pictures of me, and you will go very far."

"You are one very confident man."

"Have you not seen the way I look?"

"Yes, and you reminded me about hundred times tonight."

The waitress came back in with the drinks. Luca decided he was going to order for the both of them seeing that she never had sushi before, "make sure it's not raw, Bianca here doesn't like raw fish." The waitress smiled, "I will bring you out our most requested, cooked sushi." Nikki smiled and thanked her. They both raised their glasses and Luca made a toast, "to new beginnings and a lot of sushi." Nikki laughed and thought he was so adorable and funny.

"Oh my God, this Martini is amazing."

"Didn't I tell you? Stick with me and you will go places, wait until you try the sushi."

"Luca so really what were you in for?"

"Nothing big, they had me in for gambling and smuggling drugs. If these stupid Feds knew me at all they would know that I'm very against drugs. I hate them and they should be off our streets, but because I'm loyal and not a rat, I took one for the team."

Nikki was just called a stupid Fed she was pissed but couldn't show it. She wasn't the one who put him away, it was Mike, and now that she thought about it, *he is a stupid Fed.* She had to grin and bear it she had to take one for her team.

"The family must be grateful to you."

"Yeah, they better kiss my ass if they know what's good for them."

They both laughed and that's when the waitress walked in with their food. Nikki had a nervous smile on her face. She knew she wasn't going to like the sushi. She didn't want to make him feel bad. Luca saw the nervous look on her face.

"Oh come on Bianca it's really not that bad. I promise you; you will love it"

Luca got the chop sticks and got the first piece of sushi and tried it first to make sure it was good. "Oh my God this is to die for." He got the second piece dipped it in the special sauce and fed her. At first she pushed him away. "Come on its really good just try it." She closed her eyes and opened her mouth Luca fed her a piece of sushi. The whole time she had her eyes closed, as she started to realize she liked it she opened her eyes in shock and just looked at Luca.

"It's ok I forgive you, I know you love it."

"Oh my God Luca this is amazing, what is it?"

"You know what it doesn't matter what's in it, you like it and that's all that counts."

She got her chop sticks and started to try the other pieces. She was impressed with every new piece she tried. She just looked at Luca and he was just staring at her.

"What, am I eating it wrong?"

"No not at all, I'm just admiring you and wondering where you have been all my life."

"Oh stop, you are making me blush."

"No that would be the Martini, would you like another one?"

"No I'm good with this one, thank you."

"You really do have an amazing smile."

"Thank you."

They were sitting pretty close and Luca was just staring in her eyes. He grabbed her hand and just held it and asked her again, "where have you been all my life?" He leaned over to kiss her and she was about to kiss him until she realized what she was doing. She pushed him away and apologized.

"I'm sorry Luca I can't do this."

"What's wrong, is it something I said or did?"

"No not at all but I'm not like that, I really don't know you."

"I've been with you all night and you still don't know me?"

She couldn't help but laugh, "I don't know what kind of women you've dated but I'm not your average typical woman. I respect myself too much."

"You know what, I'm sorry. You are right. I didn't mean to be so forward. You are not the typical girl I date. You are very different and that's what I'm attracted to. I respect you for that."

"Thank you Luca, I appreciate that. I am having a really nice time but I hate to cut it short. I do have work in the morning."

"Yes of course, it's getting late and I to have to get up early."

They walked out and Luca said bye to all his buddies, "Luca come back soon." They got the car and Luca walked around to make sure there was no damage to it. He thanked the kid and gave him another twenty.

"Bianca I'm sorry if I stepped out of line, I hope you are not going home early for that?"

"No Luca it's fine, I had a really long day and I do have to get up early."

They got to Nikki's place and Luca came out of the car to open her door. This impressed her very much. Luca placed his arms around her and just stared into her eyes.

"Can I walk you upstairs?"

At first she didn't think it was a good idea but she didn't want him thinking that he did anything wrong.

"Sure, why not."

They got to her front door and she thought to herself this is as far as you go tonight. She leaned against her door and he was leaning with one arm around her waist and the other on top of the door. He couldn't stop staring into her eyes. She felt something when he stared at her and she couldn't explain it. She wanted so badly to kiss him but she had to stop feeling this way. For one he was her subject, and two she was married, what would Brian think?

"You really do have the most amazing green eyes, Bianca can I ask you something? I hope it's not too forward or too early, but I can't help but show you off to the world"

"Sure Luca what do you want to ask me?" Nikki felt like she was under a spell, she was staring at him and couldn't take her eyes off of him. Did she have one too many Martinis?

"The family is having this big welcome home party this weekend in my honor I would love it if you came with me"

"I don't know Luca meeting the family already, don't you think it's a bit too soon?"

"Not at all, I'm not letting you get away."

"I guess its fine, when is it?"

"Sunday."

She nodded and just stared into his eyes. Luca leaned in and tried to kiss her again, this time Nikki didn't stop him. They kissed for what seemed forever. He grabbed her by her waist and pulled her closer. She lost herself in his kiss she couldn't stop even if she tried. She liked it too much. He grabbed her face and held it as they were kissing. Luca had these big hands that just covered her whole face. She finally pulled herself together and pulled away.

"So much for me respecting myself."

"I'm sorry Bianca I just couldn't resist."

"It's Ok Luca, I actually liked it but this is as far as you go tonight"

"I can live with that." He smiled grabbed her face and kissed her goodnight.

"Can I call you tomorrow?"

"I don't know can you, did you lose feelings in your fingers?"

"No of course not."

"Then I don't see why you can't call."

They both smiled, "Bianca I had a great time tonight."

"So did I, thank you for introducing me to my new favorite food."

"I'm glad I can be of service to you."

Nikki opened the door and walked in, "Goodnight Luca."

"Goodnight Babe."

"Yes, goodnight babe, tonight you earned it."

Nikki walked into her new apartment. She felt weird, this wasn't her place and tonight she would be spending her first night alone. She started to explore and get used to her surroundings. Her phone rang and she jumped, "who can be calling me at this hour?"

"Nikki honey, how are you?"

"Brian how is training going?"

"Its fine, I'm just missing you very much."

Nikki was feeling a little guilty. Brian still had no clue that the operation changed and the fact that she kissed Luca made it worse. The worst part of it was that she actually enjoyed Luca when he kissed her and she couldn't stop thinking about the kiss, how it made her feel and how lost she had become in his kiss.

"Nikki are you there?"

"Yes I'm sorry Brian I just walked in from work and I'm just a little tired."

"You are getting in late."

"Yes I know things changed since you left."

"What are you talking about Nikki, what changed?"

"Brian I should've told you the day you left but I didn't want to worry you."

"Nikki you are making me really nervous, are you ok, did something happen, should I come back?"

"No Brian you don't have to leave training. I'm fine. The operation changed."

Nikki explained to Brian the new details and how she had to move out and she ran into Luca. Brian was really upset and didn't like it. He feared for her life and explained to her that this is serious and that she needed to back away from the case.

"Brian how dare you tell me that? This is my job and I worked so hard to get a case like this."

"Nikki you have to play his girlfriend and mingle with the mob, how can I NOT be upset?"

"Brian I am not having this discussion with you. You knew all this when you got involved with me. I told you then and I'm telling you now, this is my job and who I am and I will not change for anyone."

Nikki was furious with Brian she knew how much this case meant to her. She understood how worried he was, but he also knew the risks and he had to deal with them.

"Fine Nikki we will discuss this when I get back on Tuesday."

"Brian I'm not backing down so there really isn't anything to discuss."

"Nikki please be careful. You know how much I love you, and if I lost you my world wouldn't be the same."

"I love you too Brian and you know I'm always careful, plus George and Larry are outside the apartment all the time and they follow us around so you can relax."

"Ok that makes me feel a little better, get some sleep and I will talk to you tomorrow."

"Good night Brian, I love you."

"I love you too Nikki."

Nikki hung up the phone and felt very guilty but relieved at the same time. She was glad that she finally told Brian the truth. She wasn't one to lie, and keeping something this big from her husband was hurting her. She jumped in the shower, and then afterwards, made some tea which she took with her to the bedroom to enjoy before going sleep. She was exhausted but couldn't sleep. She couldn't stop thinking of Luca and she kept touching her lips and just picturing the kiss. "This is so crazy, I need to get some sleep and get my mind of this. I can't get soft and I need to concentrate." With that said she turned off the lights and went to bed.

* * * * *

LUCA WALKED INTO HIS apartment and Vinny jumped off the couch. He ran right towards Luca.

"Where's my baby and what did you do to it?"

"Oh my God relax Vin, your baby is parked and don't worry I took good care of it, thanks for letting me borrow it."

"No problem Lu, what are friends for. But if you ever peel out like that in front of me again, I will never let you use it again."

"You liked that didn't you? I bet you didn't even know the car can do that. Vin you have to enjoy it or else why the fuck did you buy it for, to keep it in the garage?"

"Whatever Lu, I'm serious. How was your date anyway?"

"Vin I met the mother of my children. She is the most amazing woman I ever met, besides my mother of course, but she's right up there with her side to side. We had a great night. Vin, she got me good, she's like a really good book, she dragged me right in and now I have to continue reading it to see where it goes and how it ends, and I think this one has a happy ending."

"Luca, do you have to compare everything to books?"

"Vin, you know how passionate I've become for books and now I have a new obsession, Bianca. What a name."

"Oh man Lu you got it really bad for her, this is making me nervous. You need to focus we have a lot shit going on."

"What are you talking about, what did I miss?"

"I got a call from the boys they want me to go to Boston to meet with the DeVito Family."

"For what Vin?"

"Luca I don't know, do you think I'm going to get whacked?"

"No why would they want you whacked? I won't have it."

"I know Lu but I can't say no."

"Listen Vin if it makes you feel better I'll take the ride with you. They can't touch you if I'm there."

"Lu you would do that for me?"

"Of course you're my buddy, my main man. But I'm telling you this better not be involving drugs. You know how much I hate dealing with that shit. When I'm boss I'm getting rid of all that."

"Lu the families will be pissed, they won't like it. It's where all the money is coming from."

"Vin, we don't have kids yet but would you want us selling this shit to other kids? The poor parents who have to deal with these kids on drugs—I don't want it on my conscience that I did that."

"I agree with you Luca but like I said, how can we say no to the boss?"

"When are we supposed to do this job?"

"In a few days, they will keep us posted."

"I hate this shit Vin, I really do, but I got your back."

* * * * *

LARRY LOOKED AT GEORGE and smiled, "Nikki is going to be one happy camper tomorrow." George knew that this would put Nikki in a really good mood,

"Should we call her and tell her?"

"No let her sleep, we have it on tape anyway she can hear it tomorrow."

"Larry you know Luca sounds pretty decent how he doesn't want to deal with the drugs—he actually has a conscience."

"Yeah, but how many people did he kill?"

"I don't know Larry. We don't have anything linking him to any of the murders."

"Come on George, he's a gangster, he broke plenty of knee caps in his time."

"Yeah you're right. Listen why don't you sleep and I'll keep a watch and then I'll wake you and we can switch."

"Ok that sounds good, but they are probably going to sleep anyway."

*   *   *   *   *

NIKKI WOKE UP IN the middle of the night in a cold sweat. She grabbed her stomach and realized she was crying. She tried to remember what she was dreaming but it was very blurry. The only thing she could remember was that it was pouring and she was in a rush to get somewhere. She couldn't understand why she woke up crying. *I really hate this why am I crying?* She thought for awhile, *Fucking sushi yeah it was good but now I'm having nightmares, I knew there was a reason I didn't like sushi.* She made herself a cup of Chamomile tea and went back to bed. She got up really early the next day as she had a lot to do but first things first, the gym. She couldn't start her day without a good work out. She also had to check in with the boys, she was sure they wanted to hear the events of the night. *Oh man I have to go buy a dress for this party on Saturday.* She stopped thinking of what she had to do and just got up to do it. She ran across to Starbucks picked up her Mocha, *I love living so close to my favorite coffee shop.* Her phone rang and at first she hoped it was Luca but realized it was too early for him.

"Larry I was just thinking of you, what do you have for me?"

"Nikki you will be happy to know that they are sending them to Boston to meet with the DeVito family."

"Really and when did you find this out?"

"Last night when Luca came back from the date, which reminds me, how did that go?"

Nikki couldn't help but touch her lips and remember the kiss.

"It was ok it was the first date, so of course he didn't really say much. Just that he took one for the team and he had nothing to do with the drugs. However, he did invite me to the party Saturday, so the plan is in motion and hopefully I can get him to trust me and tell me more."

"Good job Nikki but I'm still a little nervous about you going without any wires on Sunday, we need to get to you fast if, God forbid, someone finds you out."

"Larry I told you and the chief that I can't do that. They will be checking everyone. It's too risky and we still have so much more information we can't have our cover blown this soon."

"Ok but you know we are going to be there and ready if anything goes down."

"I should hope so. I'm heading to the gym. Just stay on sleeping beauty and let me know if anything comes up."

"How did you know he was still sleeping?"

"Larry it's six in the morning, he's probably in his twenty dreams by now."

They both laughed and hung up. Nikki was just getting in her car and her phone rang again.

"What now Larry?"

"Oh babe already you are cheating on me? Who's this Larry?"

"Luca?"

"Yeah it's me, who's this Larry guy?"

"It's my boss he was just calling to see if I was on my way in."

"Isn't it a little too early for the office?"

"Isn't it a little too early for you to be up?"

"I couldn't stop thinking of you, I couldn't sleep last night. The only thing I could think about was those gorgeous green eyes and that amazing kiss."

"Wow, I left quite an impression on you."

"Babe you have no idea what you did to me and Luca doesn't get like this."

"Then I'm really that good?"

"I don't know, I'll tell you when we cross THAT bridge."

"Yeah well you can wait for that bridge because it's going to be a long ride."

"Oh sweet thing you got a way with words."

"Sweet thing?"

"Wait I didn't earn that right yet, ok maybe our second kiss."

She couldn't help but smile.   There really was something about him and the way he talked that made her feel so giddy and like a school girl. It brought her out of her safe zone and she felt like she was invincible.

"Is everything ok Luca, why did you call?"

"Oh, do I need to an excuse to call my girl?"

"Back up there player, one night and one kiss doesn't make me your girl, so take it easy."

"Yeah, ok whatever you say, but I know you felt what I felt last night and you are officially my girl."

"Luca I need to get to the gym before work, so I will talk to you later."

"Ok, I was thinking maybe tonight we can see each other or something."

"Call me later and maybe we will."

"Sweet thing, I mean that's great, I'll call you later."

Nikki hung up and smiled. She stared at the phone and wondered where he will take her tonight. She had to snap herself back to reality. She started the car and headed to the gym. She was really into her work out when she heard Mike behind her. "You got some ass, ummm…what I would do to you." He slapped her ass and groaned. Nikki grabbed him and pinned him to the floor, she straddled him and pinned his arms down, "you ever touch me again or make another remark like that to me and I swear Mike, I will shoot you."

Mike smiled, "oh I like this better I love a woman who takes control." She got off of him, "go fuck yourself Mike the only way I would ever be with you is in your fucking dreams and in my nightmares."

Mike got up and shook it off. "You're a bitch, but I love it."

"What the fuck do you want Mike? I was having a good work out until you came."

"I could think of a few ways to make you work out."

"Go to hell asshole!"

"What's your problem?"

"You are Mike, haven't you realized that by now?"

"How's your case going I heard you had a hot date last night, what's the matter you didn't get laid?"

Nikki went to hit him but he grabbed her hand,

"Relax Nikki, I'm kidding."

"I don't like you Mike so just stay out of my face."

"Fine enjoy your work out, BITCH."

CHAPTER 10

Mike was in the office talking to the chief when Nikki walked in and sat at her desk. She was dying to know what was going on but she had some paper work to take care of and she had enough of Mike for one day.

"Chief listen I think we need to have Nikki leave the office."

"Why Mike did something happen?"

"No, I'm just saying with what's going and with her now being the gangster's girlfriend, don't you think it's best if we kept her out of the office, you know how she likes to snoop around."

"You're right Mike that is a good idea, plus we can't risk her being followed and them finding out who she is. Good thinking Mike and this has nothing to do with the fact that you two can't stand each other?"

"I wouldn't mind seeing less of that bitch around here."

"Mike that's not nice."

"Yeah, well neither is she."

Mike walked out and the chief called Nikki into the office. Nikki and Mike were face to face and she would have loved to just spit in his face, but she was a lady and just shot him a fake smile instead.

Mike laughed right back at her, "yeah you are just thinking about this morning when you were on top of me and how much you liked it."

Nikki would've loved to just take out her .38 and shoot him, but instead she punched him in the groin and continued to the office. Mike went down hard and all the guys were laughing.

"You know better than to fuck with her Mike, why do you bother?"

"Fuck you Tim go back to work and mind your fucking business." Nikki closed the door and sat down.

"Why do you torture him like that?"

"Chief he's an asshole and he has no respect for women. He's lucky I didn't shoot it off."

"How did it go last night?"

"It was ok. It was the first date so of course nothing was said, but he did invite me to the party this weekend."

"Nikki this party is making me really nervous, because going in there alone isn't a really good idea."

"Chief we went over this please let's drop it plus Larry and George won't be too far away. Is everything ok why did you call me in?"

"What are you doing here Nikki? Why are you in the office?"

"What do you mean, I'm working, I work here remember?"

"Yes of course but Nikki you can't be coming in the office now that you and Luca are somewhat of a couple. He might have you followed or one of the other guys might follow you. You can blow your cover. SO I decided that until this case is over you need to work from home. We will touch base via phone and communicate that way. Of course the guys will be in the van the whole time, but I don't want you anywhere near them, do you understand me Nikki?"

"Chief so what am I supposed to do with my time?"

"Nikki you will be working on Luca, you will work from home I just don't want you near the office. It will blow your cover."

"Ok that's fine. I have a dress to go shopping for anyway."

"See you are talking now, so go. And Nikki, I need you to touch base every morning."

"Yes Sir, will do."

"AND most important, please be careful."

"Of course boss I always am."

Nikki walked out and headed straight to her desk and took all the necessary paper work she would need to work from home. Mike was very happy and was going to say something but Tim held him back and shook his head, "why bother you are going to get shut down anyway."

He looked at Tim, "yeah you're right." Nikki didn't bother either she had so much to do. She was going to drop everything off and then go shopping for a dress. She got into her car and headed straight home. She was still thinking about the chief and Mike, she didn't know what the big case was, but she knew if Mike was involved it wasn't good, especially with those two goons that always showed up when no one was around. She had to drop the files off at her apartment she couldn't have them laying around in the new place, just in case Luca saw them. Brian was still out of town but she still had to make sure no one was watching her. She parked a block away from her place and decided to walk the rest of the way. She put the key in the lock and heard noises coming from the apartment. At first she thought she had left the TV on but she didn't want to take any chances, and got her gun ready just in case. She walked in and heard Brian in the bedroom. "You are leaving already?" Nikki was confused I thought he was in training until Tuesday? She saw a blonde girl come out of the bathroom, "What are you talking about I'm right here." The girl looked at Nikki.

"Who are you?"

"No, the question is who are you, and what are you doing in my house?"

"Your house?"

"Yes my house, are you hard of hearing?"

Brian came out of the bedroom with just his boxers, "Jess, are you talking to me?"

"No Brian she's talking to me, you know YOUR WIFE!"

"OH SHIT!"

"Brian what the fuck is going on here, you didn't tell me you were married."

Nikki sat on the couch folded her legs and arms, "Yes dear please let me in on it too, I'm dying to know myself what's going on."

"Honey, I can explain."

"Really you can because I can't see you getting out of this one, should I put on the shaggy, it wasn't me?"

Jess ran into the bedroom and got her clothes and started to get dressed. Nikki yelled to her from the couch.

"Oh Jess dear, don't forget your bra."

"Thanks, I was looking for that."

"No problem, anytime, help yourself to anything else you like, oh wait you already did MY HUSBAND!"

Jess couldn't run out of there fast enough. Brian was trying really hard to figure out how to explain this, but he knew he was caught and that he was done, not even Shaggy could help him at this point. Nikki was just sitting on the couch looking at her nails and *thought I need a manicure before Sunday.* She waited for Jess to leave so she can rip into her husband and tell him where to go.

"I'm really sorry about this I didn't know he was married. Trust me, if I knew, this wouldn't have happened."

"It was nice meeting you."

"Ah ok, you too?" Jess was confused she thought Nikki was very calm especially that she just walked in on her and her husband. She left and didn't even look back. Nikki remained on the couch and waited for her husband to start talking.

"Nikki listen I'm really sorry, but you are never home and you are always working."

"Save it Brian, and don't you dare turn this around and make it my fault. Am I supposed to feel guilty for having a career or for doing my job? If you had an issue you should've came to me and told me, not sleep with the first blonde bimbo that you run into."

"You know Nikki you were pretty calm about the whole thing."

"Calm? What the fuck did you want me to do, take her out or break her knee caps? What the fuck Brian, did you want me to go crazy and maybe cry?"

"Listen to you, you sound like one of them already"

"What the fuck are you talking about?"

"You sound like a gangster."

"That's just great Brian, turn it all around and blame me or just change the subject."

Nikki got up and walked into the bedroom and packed the rest of her things. She was leaving and not looking back. She was so hurt and dying inside but she was always the strong one and didn't want Brian to see her weakness. She held back her tears and looked at Brian right in the eyes.

"I loved you and you betrayed me. You are nothing but a RAT and there's nothing I hate more right now."

"Did your new boyfriend give you a gangster dictionary because you sure sound like one right now."

"Yeah Brian just believe that this is my fault if that's what will make you feel better. I will be back for the rest of my stuff when you are not here." Nikki grabbed her stuff and started to walk out.

"Nikki please don't leave! I love you. Let's work this out."

"Brian there isn't anything to work out, once a cheater always a cheater. I will not sit here and be played for a fool. Have a nice life." Nikki walked out and slammed the door. As soon the door closed behind her the tears just started to roll down her face. She couldn't breathe and couldn't believe what she just witnessed. How can he hurt her like that? She needed a distraction. She had to drop everything off and go shopping.

CHAPTER 11

SHE PULLED UP TO her place and parked the car. She left everything in the trunk she couldn't risk Luca seeing the files. She looked across and saw Starbucks, *I can sure use a Mocha just about now.* She walked in got her coffee and went to her apartment. The door men stopped her, "Ms. Monteleone you have a package." She wasn't expecting anything where did this package come from? "Thanks Henry." She grabbed the big white package which had D&G written across it. "I didn't order anything." She was having a really off day, but the fact that it was from D&G made her somewhat happy. She walked in, dropped the mail on the counter and put the package on the couch. She examined it just in case it wasn't what it seemed to be. "But who dropped this off? Nice Nikki there's a card why don't you pick it up and read it? Great now I'm talking in the third person and to myself." She opened the card it read:

Hey BABE Thank you for a very nice time yesterday. I enjoyed your company and looking forward to showing you off on Saturday. I'll make sure there will be plenty of sushi there for you. I hope you enjoy my little gift that I got you. I know you are going to look amazing in this and will blow everyone away. Hope to see you soon BABE!

Luca

Nikki couldn't help but smile from ear to ear. She opened the box and there was the most beautiful red strapless gown. She picked it up and put it against her to make sure it was the right size. Just as she was about to try it out her phone rang.

"Hello"

"Hey babe you miss me yet?"

Nikki was still upset about Brian and she tried to smile.

"Hi Luca."

"What's the matter? I'm not sensing your smile. Did you get my package?"

"Oh yes Luca it's gorgeous but really you didn't have to do that."

"I know I didn't, but I wanted to. I went shopping today for a suit for Sunday and I saw this gown, I knew you would wear this dress and knock them all dead. With that gorgeous golden brown mane of yours and your green eyes, everyone will be jealous."

"That's really sweet of you Luca, thank you very much I will wear it. You saved me a whole afternoon of going around looking for something to wear."

"Does that mean you have the day off?"

"Yes, I came home early today."

"That's great because I'm going to pick you up in an hour we are going to Jersey."

"What? No Luca I'm really not in the mood today."

"That word 'No' isn't in my vocabulary so get dressed, shower whatever you have to do, put on jeans, nothing dressy. I will be there in an hour."

He didn't give her a chance to respond, he hung up and she just looked at the phone. "UGH fine! I guess I can use a distraction." She threw the phone on the couch and just put her face in her hands, she started to cry. She felt like her whole world had just fallen apart but she had to pull herself together before Luca came. Larry called and touched base with her. He had heard Luca's conversation and he wanted to let Nikki know that he and George won't be too far behind, and that they will be following them. She thanked him and jumped into the shower.

Henry called from downstairs to let Nikki know that her gentleman friend was on his way up. She thanked him and hung up. Luca rang the bell she walked over and opened the door.

"There she is my green eyed beauty."

"I'm starting to think that's all you like about me."

"No way have you seen yourself, you are HOT."

"Like I said you have a way with words. So where are we going, and why was I told to wear jeans?"

"Oh, come here, no kiss?"

"What?"

Luca walked over to Nikki grabbed her by her waist, pulled her really close and looked into her eyes, "Where's my kiss?" He kissed her and she got all weak in the knees. He sensed she wasn't herself.

"What's wrong Bianca?"

"Nothing."

"Bianca you are lying to me. Tell me what's wrong."

Nikki pulled away and walked away from Luca. She got her bag and keys and was ready to go. "So where are we going?"

"Bianca you are lying to me." Nikki couldn't understand how he knew she was lying. She was smiling and didn't have any tears in her eyes.

"Luca I'm fine, let's go"

"I know you're lying because you looked left and changed the subject TWICE"

"What the fuck are you talking about?"

"Let me teach you a little trick. You know when someone is lying by the eye test."

"The eye test, have you totally lost your mind?"

"It's simple. When I asked you if there was something wrong your eyes went straight to the left, which means a lie. Then I asked you again and you changed the subject, that's a straight lie."

"Ok, so if I looked right instead of left that would mean what, that you are a crazy man?"

"You are so funny, no it would mean you were telling the truth."

"Luca you are making me crazy, can we please go now?"

"Fine but you lied and I know something is bothering you."

Nikki grabbed Luca's face and looked at him straight in the eyes, "I had a bad day at work."

"Ok that's true."

She threw her hand up "I give up," and walked out of the apartment.

They got in the car and started to drive. Nikki was looking out the window and was thinking of Brian and how he betrayed her. She was so hurt but she couldn't show it. Brian kept texting her and tried to call her few times but she had the phone on silent so that Luca couldn't hear it. She thought to herself, "I wish I knew the eye test before so I could've used it on Brian." Luca was talking but she didn't hear one word he was saying.

"OH, Bianca I'm talking to you."

"I'm sorry Luca I was just thinking of work."

"What's wrong with work?"

She had to think of something quick, "they want me to take scenic pictures of the fall tress and the season but I would have to leave town to find that. Yes, New York has pretty places but the leaves are already gone and winter is coming faster than we all thought."

"I have an idea me and Vinny are going to Boston in a few days on business why don't you come along? While we are at our meeting you can go to the public gardens and take some really nice pictures."

"Wow you know about the public garden?"

"Doesn't everyone?"

"Hey that's my line. I love Boston it's one of my favorite places to visit especially when my New York Yankees are playing The Red Socks."

"Well then it's settled, you are coming with us and the Yankees are playing there Wednesday. I'll get tickets so we can go watch the game."

"I don't know Luca I don't want to be the third wheel with you and your friend."

"Oh please, like Vinny is going to mind, he'll bring one of his girls and we'll make it a nice weekend out of it."

"Let's just play it by ear and see what happens."

As she was finishing up her sentence she turned and he was pulling into the horseback riding place. Nikki's mouth dropped. She loved horseback riding and she hasn't gone since she was a kid. Luca saw the expression on her face.

"Please tell me you like horseback riding?"

"Oh my God Luca I love it! I haven't gone since I was a little girl, my dad used to take me all the time. What made you come here?"

"I have been away for four years and I miss my horse, so this is the next best thing."

Nikki got out of the car before he had a chance to open her door. She was like a kid in a candy store. She noticed that when she was with Luca she was this wild and free woman. She felt like she hadn't a care in the world. She would forget that this was work, and every once in a while she had to remind herself. The owner came up to them, and of course like the rest of the world he knew Luca.

"Luca my boy how have you been, when did you get out?"

"A few days ago"

Mi, Luca che bella ma chi e? Nikki understood Italian and the man was asking Luca who she was. Nikki answered him instead

"Ciao, Bianca Monteleone, piacere."

Luca's mouth just dropped open, he was very impressed that Bianca understood and could speak Italian. He thought to himself *where has she been all my life.*

"Luca she's beautiful and she speaks better Italian than you, *Ciao* Bianca my name is Tony."

"It's a pleasure to meet you Tony."

"You kids ready to ride? The trails are closed today, but for you we make exceptions."

"That's my man Tony." He put his arm around Tony, "I missed you Tony, how's the family? Everyone ok?"

"Thank God everyone is doing fine."

Tony picked out the best two horses and walked them over. Luca looked at Tony;

"Tony one horse so I can get close to my girl here."

Tony smiled at him, "Whatever you want Luca, and if its romance you want make sure you ride by the beach."

Tony helped Nikki get on first and made sure she was comfortable. Luca got on behind her.

Nikki looked back at Luca, "Back up there cowboy you are a little too close."

"What's the matter babe I'm turning you on?"

"Don't flatter yourself, I like my space."

"Oh but the whole point was for me to be right up behind you."

He grabbed her by her waist and squeezed her tight; "you are just nervous because you might just like it." She didn't let him see her, but she was smiling, and she did like it. Tony looked at the both of them, "Like I said the trails are closed, the place is as secluded as you want it." Luca shook his hand, "Thanks Tony we will take advantage." Before he could finish the sentence Nikki slapped the reins on the horse and the horse took off flying. Luca almost fell off the horse for that was how fast she made the horse take off.

"OH, BABE you are going to knock me off the horse."

"That was the plan, but I guess it didn't work."

"Oh sweet thing you wouldn't want that."

She smiled and Luca was pressing himself against her and holding her by the waist. Nikki was enjoying it but he really did need to back away, she was getting a little excited. He felt her, he knew what she was feeling, and he couldn't understand how this woman got this hold on him. No woman has ever been able to do that.

"You really know how to ride this horse."

"Oh, you have no idea how well I can ride it."

"If I didn't know any better, I'd think you are talking dirty and nasty to me. I like it."

"Your mind is always on one thing isn't it?"

"Yes and lately it's been on you, I can't seem to get you off my mind."

They came up to the beach and Nikki pulled on the reins so the horse would stop. Luca jumped off first and then helped Nikki down. He grabbed her from the waist and she jumped off. He must've been off balance because they both fell to the floor and Nikki ended up on top of Luca.

"Oh I see, now you want to ride me."

"Oh stop." She was going to get off him but he held her down.

"Don't get off, stay here." He lifted himself up and started to kiss her. Her hair was all over him and he couldn't help but pull it away from her face. He held her face and she was still on top of him. He looked at her in the eyes, "you really are beautiful." He continued to kiss her and she was weak and lost, she didn't want to stop, but she was falling for him and she couldn't. This was not what was supposed to happen. He was supposed to be this bad gangster who was going to be put away for life for all the wrong he had done, but she couldn't find one thing to hold against him. The only thing she was learning was that this man was decent and sincere. She finally pulled away and looked in his eyes she realized that she really liked this man. She looked up and noticed that on the beach someone had set up a blanket and there was a picnic basket with two glasses and a bottle of wine being chilled. She got off of Luca.

"Babe, where are you going?"

"Luca look someone left a picnic basket." Luca smiled, he got up and walked behind her.

"Well what do you know, how did they know we were hungry?"

"You planned this? But how did you know I would say yes?"

"Oh come on I told you 'no' doesn't exist in my vocabulary."

They went to sit down on the blanket and Luca poured the wine. They lifted their glasses and Luca made a toast; "To new beginnings and a happy ending." They drank and then Luca kissed her. "So are you hungry?"

She looked in the basket, "I'm starving what did you pack?"

"I don't know. Let's see what Tony made us." Tony knew Luca very well, so he packed his favorite, grilled chicken Cesar salad for two, and some fresh cheese with whole wheat bread. He also packed some fresh strawberries and homemade whipped cream. "Tony knows me too well."

"How do you know Tony?"

"He's an old family friend. He and my father used to work together."

"Really, doing what?'

"You know the family business."

"And that would be what?"

"You want some cheese?"

"Ah you changed the subject so you are lying."

"Oh so now you are going to use what I taught you against me?"

"It was a mistake telling me your little eye test secret, now I'll know when you are lying."

"I have no reason to lie to you. Tony and my dad were cousins and they grew up together. They worked the family business together. My dad took a bullet for Tony and he feels he owes it to me for the rest of his life."

"Like father like son."

"Yes everyone tells me I'm just like my father. I believe in the same things my dad did. He was an honest and loyal man. He's the one who taught me to hate rats and never let the family down"

"I can see in your eyes that you looked up to your father."

"I did. He taught me everything I know and I try not to disappoint him. I know he's looking down on me."

"And I'm sure he would be proud of you. So tell me Luca what are you going to Boston for? What kind of business do you have there?"

"You know you ask a lot of questions."

"I'm just trying to get to know you better."

"Let's talk about you, what really got you upset today?"

Why did he have to go and remind her of what happened. She was just finally starting to forget about what Brian did to her and he had to go and bring it all up again. Her eyes went down and she stopped smiling. Luca picked up her chin, "It can't be that bad." She forced a smiled and made sure she looked at him straight in the eyes, now that she knew about the eye test she didn't want to give anything away.

"Really it was just work, my boss doesn't appreciate the work I do, and I'm good at what I do."

"You want me to take care of this guy for you?" Nikki laughed.

"No, I don't want you to take care of him, I'm a big girl and I can handle it myself."

"I'm sure you can, but sometimes it doesn't hurt to ask for help."

"Well thank you, but no thanks. So you still didn't answer my question, what business do you have in Boston?"

"I'm going to meet with some of the families, I've been away for four years and I have some catching up to do."

"I see, you have some skeletons in your closet?"

"No I'm pretty much an open book, what you see is what you get."

"Speaking of books, have you read any good books lately?"

"Actually my favorite author just came out with a new book and I want to go pick it up"

"And who is that?"

"Giovanni Gambino, he came out with Prince of Omerta it got some great reviews."

"You really like to read, I wouldn't think you were a reader."

"Being away you have to do something. I had to stay out of trouble, so I got into reading. I was actually going to write a book on my experience in the joint."

"Wow, and what does the family think about that?"

"They don't know yet, I haven't mentioned it, but what's it to them anyway?"

"I don't know, I just thought you guys were really private people."

"We are but who says I have to write secrets?"

"I guess you got a point."

"I know I do."

They finished their lunch and packed everything up. Luca said to leave everything and Tony's guys would pick it up later. He helped her up on the horse but this time Nikki got behind him and let him ride the horse. She wrapped her arms around him and held on tight. He liked it that her arms and legs were wrapped around him. They just enjoyed the ride and didn't speak much. They thanked Tony for the great afternoon got in the car and left. As they pulled up to Nikki's place Luca put the car in park and just stared at her.

"What?"

"Nothing I'm admiring your beauty."

"Thank you Luca for such a wonderful afternoon. After the morning I had it really hit the spot"

"I'm glad I can be of service to you. Listen I have some business to take care of tonight but maybe afterwards I can swing by for a nightcap?"

"As tempting as that sounds, I don't think I'm ready for that yet."

"Babe we don't have to do anything."

"I know, but noticing the chemistry between us we will, and I'm not ready for that. I just came out of a relationship and I still need some time to heal."

"I can respect that."

He walked out and opened the door for Nikki. She came out and he held her. "I don't want to leave you, but I have to." They kissed for a long time. Nikki pulled away, "I really have to go I have some work I need to finish". He nodded and smiled at her.

"Thanks again for taking the ride with me."

"No Luca, thank you for taking me and making me forget the horrible morning I had."

He waited for her to go up and he got in the car and left.

CHAPTER 12

LUCA PULLED UP TO his place and found Vinny waiting for him. He looked really pissed. Luca got out of his car and just laughed;

"Vin you need to get laid, you always look worried and miserable, what's up with that?"

"Lu where the fuck have you been all day, I've been waiting for hours?"

"Vin I know I've been away for four years but they did invent cell phones, you could've used yours to call me and find out where I was."

"I didn't see you pick up your phone and call me."

"I'm sorry Vin I didn't know we were in that stage of our relationship where I had to tell you every move I make."

"Where were you?"

"I was with Bianca. We went horseback riding, we had an amazing time. Vin have I mentioned that she's going to be the mother of my children?"

"Yeah, like a million times. Lu you are getting too close to her. Do you even know anything about her?"

"What is there to know that she's amazing, gorgeous, the most beautiful person I ever met oh and of course she's going to be the mother of my children?"

Vinny threw his hands up, "I give up. I think I rather you start talking about books again".

"What's wrong Vin, why are you cranky?"

"You said we were going to see Mr. B today, and here I am waiting for you and you're out romancing the future mother of your children."

"Relax Vin we are going to see Mr. B and I said later anyway. I just need to go up shower and we can go. Oh by the way Bianca is coming to Boston with us."

"What? Are you really losing your mind, do you trust her that much?"

"Vin, I don't know what it is about her but I would trust her with my life. We connected in a way that I can't even explain. Plus while you are doing your business me and Bianca are going to watch a game and just hang out."

"Maybe because you've been in the joint for so long you think the first chic comes along and bang she's it."

"No she's different, and I just have a really good feeling about her. I figured you can ask one of your bimbos to tag along, what do you think?"

"I don't know, it is business we are going up there for."

"Oh lighten up you only live once you might as well enjoy it."

"Just go take a shower Mr. B is waiting."

Luca and Vinny went upstairs. Vinny sat on the couch while waiting for Luca to finish getting ready. Luca told him how great Tony looked and what a great day they had. Vinny just kept shaking his head. He never had seen Luca like this before. Luca wasn't one to get attached to women. He always said he wouldn't get emotionally involved because at the end they end up hurting you. So Vinny was seeing a new side of his friend that he thought ever existed.

Luca came out of the shower and looked at Vinny, "Oh, we have to go, get off your ass." He wanted to talk to Mr. B about this Boston trip. Luca wasn't into the drug business he thought it was wrong and that he didn't want to be the one fucking up people's life. So this meeting was to express his feeling about what he intended to tell the other families when he became the boss.

Vinny looked at Luca in shock, "what the fuck I have been waiting for you all day and now you are in a rush?"

Luca looked at Vinny, "the sooner we go the sooner we get back and maybe I get to see my girl again. Vin, what did she do to me? I can't stop thinking about her, it's like she put a spell on me or something."

Vinny just shook his head, "Luca those are the ones you have to stay away from, they will fuck your mind up and stomp on your heart, leaving it in a million pieces."

Luca was speechless, "oh stop watching Doctor Phil you are really starting to scare me. Come on Mr. B is waiting." They got in the car and headed over to the boss' house. Luca was just staring out the window and thinking about Bianca and the day they had. Even though he joked about what Vinny had said, he knew that his friend was right and he was afraid that he would get his heart broken. He didn't know what it was, but there was a connection with Bianca. Vinny pulled up to Mr. B's and they both got out.

"Lu you need to snap out of it, you look like you are in another world."

"Vin, I'm good, don't worry about me. When it comes to business I'm here."

"Ok good, 'cause you are starting to worry me."

Mr. B was in his office waiting for them. He was just getting off the phone when they walked in. He motioned for the boys to sit down and said good bye on the phone.

"Boys how are you? That was Carlo DeVito he's looking forward to seeing you in Boston."

Luca cleared his throat and looked at Vinny. Mr. B realized that Luca had something on his mind and told him to just let it out. "It's funny you bring up Boston that's what I wanted to speak about. I decided to take the ride up there with Vinny. The Yankees are playing the Soxs and I thought I can use the ride. There are also a few things I had on my mind. Mr. B you've known me a long time, and you know that I'm very much like my father and like him I'm really not into this drug trafficking. I know that families rely on this for most of the income, but I was hoping that maybe after I become boss we can do something else."

"My dear Luca you know the families will not be too happy about this but what did you have in mind?"

"Well I have a few things in the works and I rather wait to see how they pan out before I start pitching my ideas."

"I know you Luca, and I know you are a very smart man and you will do very well for the families, and that's why I chose you to take my place. But I still need you to go to Boston Wednesday to meet with Carlo."

"Yes and we will boss, you know we never let you down."

"That's my boy. So are you boys ready for the big party this weekend? Luca you are bringing a date?"

Vinny couldn't hold back he had to put his two cents in.

"Oh yeah, he's bringing the mother of his children."

"Oh really who is this girl? Is she from the family?"

"No Boss, you know I never mix business with pleasure."

"Luca someone we can trust, right?"

"Yeah of course she's harmless. Just don't look at her in her big green eyes 'cause you will be struck by lighting."

"Well I'm looking forward to meeting her Luca. OK boys, I have some stuff to do for this big weekend.

"Ok boss sounds like a plan."

They all said their goodbyes and Vinny and Luca left.

CHAPTER 13

NIKKI JUST SAT IN the van with the headset on smiling as she heard Luca talk to Mr. B about not liking the drug business. She knew that he had some good in him and she couldn't help but think about the day she spent with him and how he made her forget about Brian. George looked at her and knew she was falling for him.

"So you never told us how your day went with Luca today"

"It was actually nice he isn't your typical gangster."

"If I didn't know any better I say you like him."

"Oh shut up George you only have one thing on your mind."

"I'm just asking, what did you find out"

"Pretty much what he said to Mr. B, that he's going to Boston as a matter of fact he wants me to go with them."

Larry looked at her, "You didn't tell us that"

"I didn't?"

"No you didn't, do you actually think that is a good idea?"

"Yes of course, I can see what they are doing and of course you guys will not be too far from us"

"I agree but Nikki I'm getting a little nervous about all this and then this weekend is this huge party I'm afraid you will be found out."

"Larry you need to stop worrying about me, I have faith in you guys and that you will be there for me if anything happens."

"Of course we will be but I don't have to be ok with it."

"Larry you're great you're like the brother I never had."

George a little offended, "What about me?"

"George you are like a hemorrhoid, a big pain in my butt."

"Gee, thanks a lot Nikki."

"Anytime George."

Nikki had a long day and decided to call it a night. She left the boys in charge and instructed them to call her if anything interesting happened. She had every intention of just going home and making some dinner. On her way she decided to stop by the grocery store to pick up some food, she had this urge for Italian tonight. She was born and raised Italian so her mom taught her how to cook some of the best Sicilian dishes. She was in the mood for some Pasta Sicilian, eggplant with fresh tomatoes sautéed with garlic and oil and some fresh *ricotta salata.* Just the thought of it made her mouth water. She got everything she needed and left. As she was cooking she couldn't help but think about Brian and what he did to her. Her feelings were so confused she wasn't sure if she was hurt or just relieved. Brian and Nikki did have a great relationship but they never spent time together. Between him being at the firehouse all the time, and her being on cases and stake outs, they never really were together.

Regardless, she was very hurt. She was also thinking about Luca and how they connected. She felt more of a connection with Luca than Brian. As she was thinking of him, her phone rang.

"Hello?"

"Hey babe, were you thinking of me?" Nikki was speechless because she was, and how the heck did he know?

"Well actually I was just cooking, and yes, I was thinking about my day and you happen to be in my thoughts."

"Yeah I know I felt you."

"What?"

"I felt you, I was thinking of you too. You said you were cooking, what are you making?"

"Oh Luca you are so funny, I happen to be an amazing cook"

"Really, so what are you making me for dinner?"

"For you reservations, for me I'm making some *Pasta Alla Norm*."

"WOW Sicilian! How about I bring over some white Piemonte Moscato and we call it a date?"

Just as he was finishing the sentence there's a knock on her door, more like a bang. She wasn't expecting anyone. The only people who knew she was there was the team. She froze and thought something happened.

"Babe what's that banging?"

"Someone is at my door."

"Oh I see you already have a date coming over."

"No I don't, I'm actually not expecting anyone. Hold on while I get the door." She walked over and the banging was just getting louder and louder. "Hold your horses I'm coming!" Luca was still on the phone and he loved that she used "horses" especially after the day they had. She opened the door and saw Brian standing there completely wasted.

"Brian?"

"Babe, who the fuck is Brian?' Nikki completely forgot that Luca was still on the phone, "Luca I have to call you back."

"Brian what are you doing here?"

"Honey please, I'm begging you, I love you so much. My life is nothing without you."

"Brian you are drunk, so please leave."

"I'm not leaving honey, I'm so sorry I didn't mean to cheat on you but you were never home. You are always working and always with Larry and George."

Nikki thought she had hung up on Luca but she had her earpiece and didn't realize that he was listening to the whole conversation. Luca was flipping out, "who the fuck is this Brian and LARRY AND GEORGE? Who is she?"

"Brian I suggest you turn your drunk ass around and go back to the little bimbo you were with today!"

"Baby I need you, I'm so horny and I miss you so much. You are everything to me. If you didn't put your job before us, you would know that."

"You knew my job before we got married and you were fine with it, but you decided you wanted a little toy on the side. So why don't you go to her and get it from her?" Luca was shocked, "SHE'S MARRIED?"

Brian started to get in her face and started to grab her. "Brian, get your hands off of me!" Nikki was trying to fight him off but the more she would tell him the more he would attack her.

"Baby you know you want it and I need you, I want to fuck the shit out of you and make you scream."

Now Luca really became crazy, and he had enough of this shit. He got his keys and took off to her apartment. He feared that this stupid son of a bitch was going to hurt her. He tried to get her attention but she took her earpiece off when she thought she had hung up but Luca could still hear everything.

"Brian stop it now, or I will fucking hurt you!"

"Come on honey you know you want it and you know how great we are together." Brian ripped her shirt and she let out a huge yelp.

Luca ran every red light he didn't give a shit. No one was going to hurt his woman.

"Brian I am warning you, if you know what's good for you get the fuck off of me!" backing away, she tripped over the coffee table and fell to the floor. Brian found his opportunity and just smiled predatorily, "Well look at this, no Larry and George to help. What's wrong they have no tabs on you here in your new place. Doesn't your job require some surveillance, on the floor and helpless, poor Nikki?" Luca was so confused. "Nikki, George and Larry but who the fuck are all these people?" Brian got on his knees and proceeded to get on top of Nikki.

Luca heard Nikki trying to fight Brian off, "hold on Babe I'm coming."

Nikki couldn't hear Luca. Brian started to pull her jeans off, and she was just beating him up. He started to touch Nikki and she screamed. Nikki was no weak little girl so she used every skill she learned to fight him off. However, Brian was also very strong and had some intense training himself, but Nikki was tough and she knew how to fight him off. Brian tried really hard to pin her down and she let him think he was winning just so she could beat the shit out of him. Just when he thought that she gave up fighting she kicked him in the groin and elbowed him on his chest. He rolled off of her and she punched him in the face giving him a bloody lip.

"I told you never to fuck with me Brian." Brian started to wipe his mouth, "thank God you didn't have your gun on you."

Just as she was getting up Luca came storming in the house, "GET YOUR FUCKING HANDS OFF OF HER!" Nikki was so confused,

"Luca what are you doing here?"

"Bianca, are you ok?"

"Yes I'm fine but what are you doing?"

"You didn't hang up your phone and I heard this fucking animal put his hands all over you." Brian was a little dizzy and still bleeding.

"Oh so is this your new project, BIANCA, what, are you sleeping with him?"

"Listen buddy, I suggest you get your bloody drunk ass out of here before I finish you up."

"Wow, listen to you, what a gangster." Luca was getting really pissed and was ready to beat the fuck out of Brian. Nikki stepped in before more information could come out of Brian's mouth and ruin the whole operation. As a matter of fact she was worried now about what else Luca heard when she was fighting with Brian.

"Ok enough boys! Brian you need to leave now!" Nikki called the door man downstairs and asked him to get a cab for Brian as he was in no condition to drive.

"Fine I will leave, but Nikki this is not over!" Luca looked at Bianca with a confused expression, "Nikki?"

Nikki was ready to beat the crap out of Brian, "Just leave Brian there's a cab downstairs waiting for you." Brian blew her a kiss and pointed his fingers shaped like a gun towards Luca.

Luca just smirked, "yeah, ok buddy bring it on, anytime." Luca slammed the door in his face and turned to Nikki.

"Babe, are you ok or should I call you Nikki?" Luca took of his jacket to give to Nikki because she was shirtless. She had forgotten that Brian ripped her shirt off.

"Oh thank you but I can go get a shirt from the bedroom."

"Why did he call you Nikki?" She remembered the eye test so she had to make him believe her. She looked at him straight in the eyes, "my full name is Bianca Nicole Monteleone. Brian always called me Nikki because my mom called me Nikki. Being Italian you should know that Italian people usually use their middle names instead of their first. I prefer Bianca so I go by Bianca. My parents and Brian are really the only ones who call me Nikki."

"Well I like Bianca better, it's exotic and pure." Nikki went into her bedroom and got a clean shirt from her closet, relieved for her fast thinking.

"So Luca tell me again why you are here?"

"I was on with you and you thought you had hung up but you didn't and I heard the whole conversation. So when I heard the son of a bitch rip your shirt off, I ran over here." Nikki came out buttoning her shirt and looking up at him,

"You need to know that I can handle myself and don't need a man to fight for me."

"I can see that, you really fucked him up you are my kind of woman." He grabbed her closer and kissed her, "I have to confess I was really scared that I wasn't going to get here on time. I know we don't know each other long enough but I have this need to protect you. I have this connection with you that I can't explain."

"I know Luca I feel the same way and it makes me a little nervous."

"Why?"

"Because I never felt like this for anyone before."

"Oh sweet thing me too," he kissed her again, "Now you need to tell me who the fuck is Brian, Larry and George." Nikki laughed, "how about I tell you over dinner?"

"That's right you made some delicious pasta, which by the way you have to tell me how you did it."

"Why, you cook?"

"Yes, I love to cook it's one of my many talents."

"Really and what are the others?"

"Well, maybe after dinner I can show you."

"Easy there cowboy, you are getting way ahead of yourself."

"Ok so let's get cooking babe, show me what you're making. Tell me step by step how to make *Pasta Alla Norm.*"

"I thought you knew how to cook, *Pasta Alla Norm* is very simple; you should be able to do it with your eyes closed."

"I can, I just want to see if you are the great cook you claim to be Bianca Nicole Monteleone." Nikki led Luca to the kitchen and continued to prepare her dinner which she had started when Brian came.

"Ok well it's pretty simple, I already chopped up the eggplants into cubes, you can actually fry them but being the health freak I am, I actually put them in the oven. I place them on a cookie sheet, season with some Italian seasoning and drizzle them with some oil. When they are tender than I take them out. They should be ready by now."

Luca was right behind her looking over her shoulder, finding it very sexy watching her cook. He had his arms around her waist and started to kiss her neck. Nikki was getting really distracted and hot at the same time. She had such an urge for him, but she had to remind herself over and over again that he was just a subject.

"Ah Luca I can't cook like this, you are very distracting. Here let me get you a glass of wine." Nikki walked over to the cupboard to get Luca a glass and some wine, he was all over her. She tried to control him and started to cook again. Again he stood behind her watching her cook. "Ok so now that the eggplant is ready you sauté some garlic and oil in a skillet, throw in some chopped fresh tomatoes, throw in the eggplant some salt pepper and don't forget your fresh basil." Luca loved every minute of it but he wasn't paying attention at all.

"Um Babe it smells so good." She smiled and tried really hard not to turn around and kiss him. She wanted him but she was fighting it. "While this is cooking we can put the pot on for the pasta and get that ready. Once the pasta is cooked we drain it and put in the skillet with eggplant, this should take about ten minutes." She turned around to grab her glass of wine and Luca was right there, he gave her the biggest and longest kiss. "You know I can't help picturing you when I walked in and you had nothing but your bra on, how about I see that again?"

Nikki was still in shock from the kiss, "that won't be happening tonight."

Luca smiled and kissed her again, "Oh babe you are dealing with the master."

Nikki laughed right back at him, "You have more of a chance leaving with blue balls than seeing my bra again." With that said the pot started to boil over, she jumped and took the cover off.

Luca couldn't help but smile, "Wow you are good, you got the pot all excited too, it came out all over the place."

"Yeah that's about the only thing that will be coming out all over the place tonight."

"Ouch that really hurt."

"Keep it up and you will be leaving like Brian, with a bloody lip."

"Oh Babe you turn me on when you talk violent, you can beat me up all you want. Go ahead hurt me baby."

Nikki tried not to but she couldn't help but laugh.

He grabbed her and kissed her again, he looked straight into her eyes, "where have you been all my life?"

She looked right at him, "I've been waiting for you to come and find me." They kissed again. The pasta was ready, so she drained it and mixed it with the ingredients in the skillet. She then spooned it onto the plates and grated some *ricotta salata* on top of each plate. They brought it over to the table and Luca grabbed his glass and made a toast, "to new and better things." Nikki raised her glass and smiled. Luca took the first bite and was in heaven.

"Oh my God this is just like my mother used to make it, you are a good cook."

Nikki smiled, "Thank you."

"Now can you tell me who Brian, Larry and George are? I'm starting to think you have your own entourage here."

"Brian is my soon to be ex-husband, I found him with another woman. Larry and George are the partners of where I work."

"I didn't know you were married."

"Separated and now getting divorced. What else did you hear?"

"What did you want me to hear?"

"I'm just asking."

"Why would he say that Larry and George would have you under surveillance?"

"One cause he was drunk, and two because I'm always working and they know every move a make because of the projects they send me on."

"Like what?"

"You know you ask too many questions. Why don't you put some food in your mouth that will keep you quiet for awhile?"

"I know what can keep me quiet for awhile."

"Yeah well that's not happening, and I am NOT quiet when it comes to that."

"Wow I think you had too much wine. I was actually thinking that if I had some more wine that will shut me up but I like your idea better."

Nikki blushed, she was a little on the tipsy side and was afraid that tonight might go further than she expected. They finished their dinner and Luca helped Nikki clean help. "You are very handy in the kitchen." Luca turned Nikki around put his hand on her neck and worked his whole hand down her chest, "you have no idea how handy I am in the bedroom." Nikki was hot for him. She wasn't sure if she can resist him. She wanted him really bad but she had to back down. "Why don't we go on the couch and have some wine." Luca kissed her and while holding her he brought her to the couch. He laid her down and got on top of her. They started to get all hot and steamy. His hands were all over her. He started to unbutton her blouse, caressed her breast and started to kiss her neck. He pulled himself up and just admired her. He kissed her neck again and started to work his way down to her chest. She couldn't resist him anymore. Her shirt was off, she got up and decided to she was going to be on the top. Luca loved it very much. "I love a woman who takes charge." She continued to kiss him and his hands were on her waist, her hair was all over him and he pulled it back and looked at her straight in her eyes, "you are one amazing woman." She was in heat and she couldn't stop. He started to unbutton her jeans and that's when it hit her, "what am I doing?"

Luca continued, "You are driving me crazy, that's what you are doing." She stopped and got off of him. Luca stood there in shock, "oh, what are you doing?"

She looked at him with regret, "I'm so sorry I can't do this."

"Why not is my breath full of garlic?"

"You're so stupid, no, it's not that."

"Then what's wrong?"

"I just feel it's too soon, and after all that happened tonight, I just don't want to drag you into my mess."

"No babe, drag me in don't worry, now come here and get back on top of me." Nikki laughed and started to dress herself.

"You are too funny, is that all that's on your mind?"

"You know to be honest lately the only thing on my mind has been you and I can't get you out of it."

"Well I'm flattered but tonight is not going to be the night. I'm sorry I led you on but I'm just not ready for this."

He got up held her by her waist and kissed her. "I respect you Bianca and if you're not ready than you're not ready but you seemed pretty hot tonight."

She gave him a light tap on his face, "You are really different than I expected."

She kissed him. "I really like you Bianca, I really don't know what you did to me, but I'm looking forward to tomorrow to see what lies ahead for us." She got his jacket thanked him again for coming by. He thanked her for dinner and promised to talk to her tomorrow. "You weren't kidding when you said you were sending me home with blue balls."

She laughed so hard, "Yes I told you I would and let me tell you a secret, I did that so when you lay awake tonight in your bed, I will be the only thing on your mind."

He smiled, "you really are my kind of woman. Listen, get some sleep because tomorrow morning we are heading to Boston." She nodded and they kissed and said goodnight.

CHAPTER 14

NIKKI WOKE UP IN a cold sweat. She had the same dream as the other night. She was driving in the rain and all of sudden her car came to a stop she got out and screamed LUCA NO! She couldn't make sense of the dream but this was the second time and it really bothered her. She shook it off and decided to get up and pack a few things for Boston. Luca was picking her up in a few hours and she was actually a little excited. She was looking forward to taking a few pictures and she hadn't done that in a while. She got out her camera and made sure she had everything. She had to play it off that this was her job and if something was missing he could suspect something. She put on a pot of her favorite Starbucks coffee and started to get herself together, then touched base with Larry to make sure he was on his toes and that he wouldn't be too far. She knew Luca wouldn't do anything but, she had heard a lot about the DeVito's and they were huge with drugs. Luca might not know why they were heading up there but Nikki had a pretty good idea that something big was going to go down. All she kept thinking to herself was how she has fallen for this man in just a few days. "How can that be? This can't be normal, or is this what happens when you truly meet the one you love? But love is such a strong word, I can't possibly love him. Oh dear Lord I'm talking to myself AGAIN!" She had to call the chief and check in. He wasn't too happy about it but she insisted. She would report back everything when she got back. Just as she was hanging up with the chief she got a knock on the door.   She looked at the time and realized that it was Luca. Nikki walked over to the door and let him in.

"Have I told you how beautiful you are?"

"I can't believe you got up this early."

"I'm a morning person I get up at the crack of dawn."

"Well you should've come earlier to help me pack. I have a pot of coffee on, you want some?"

"Vinny is downstairs having a fit, we can pick up some coffee on the way up or better yet we can stop at Cracker Barrel for some breakfast."

"Oh Wow that's my favorite place, I haven't been there in awhile. That sounds like a great idea."

"Good so where is your stuff? I'll bring it down." Nikki pointed to three bags and Luca just looks at her like she's nuts.

"You know we are going for two days right?"

"One bag is my camera and my work equipment and the rest, well, I'm a woman, I have a lot of stuff."

Luca picked up the bags, "What the fuck did you pack Bricks?"

Nikki laughed, "No I couldn't decide on shoes." Luca rolled his eyes, "I will never understand women and their obsession with shoes."

Nikki pushed him out the door, "Oh shut up, Vinny is downstairs waiting and I'm getting hungry." She locked the door and they went downstairs. Vinny was outside of the car smoking a cigarette.

Luca gave him a dirty look, "you still doing that shit? I thought you would've quit that shit by now." Vinny threw out the cigarette and helped Nikki with her bag. She smiled and said hello.

"That's right, you guys haven't officially met. Bianca this is Vinny."

"Hi Vinny it's a pleasure to finally meet you, Luca is always talking about you."

"Yeah, I'm sure he has nothing nice to say. It's nice to finally meet you too. Wow you do have really nice green eyes."

Luca glared at Vinny, "Oh keep your eyes to yourself, she's mine."

"Oh really? I didn't know I was a possession."

"No babe, you are more like my obsession." He grabbed her and kissed her and she kissed him right back, smiling up at him. Vinny rolled his eyes, "Oh God, are you two going to be like this for the next two days?"

"What's the matter Vin you jealous? I thought you were going to bring one of your girls with you what happened, no one wanted to come?"

"Luca you're an ass. You know I'm not going for pleasure and that this is all business."

"Yeah, nobody wanted to come." Luca laughed and grabbed the keys, "I'm driving because I want to get there sometime this year."

Nikki laughed and got in the back seat. Luca gave her a look, "Babe you belong in the front with me."

"No it's ok, I like it back here. I didn't get much sleep and I just want to close my eyes and take a little nap."

"I want to see those gorgeous green eyes."

"Well these green eyes are tired, so Vinny you get in the front."

"Fine, you nap and I'll talk to Vinny." Vinny looked at Nikki with mock insulted expression, "I just met you. What did I ever do to you that you are sticking me in the front to deal with him?"

Nikki laughed, "I like him." Luca looked at the both of them, "Oh take it easy both of you, or you will both walk to Boston."

They all got in the car and Luca started the car and took off. It was at least four hours before they would be in Boston, but the way Luca was driving they would be up there in two. They made their pit stop at Cracker Barrel for breakfast. Vinny decided to drive the rest of the way up so Luca got in the back with Nikki. Vinny was a little upset, "oh what the fuck I look like, car service?"

Luca hugged Nikki and told Vinny to shut up and drive. He looked at Nikki and smiled, "Did you miss me?"

"Ah we have been together the whole time."

"Yeah, but I was driving and now you are in my arms." Vinny rolled his eyes, "Oh dear Lord, why me?"

"Yo Vin I'm doing you the favor and taking the ride with you, so shut the fuck up and drive."

Just as he said that Luca's phone rang. He answered it and it was Mark, the producer for Mulberry to Rome.

"Luca my man how the heck are you?"

*"*Mark I'm good, what can I do for you?"

"I'm calling to touch base with you about the movie and that we pretty much have the whole cast. We are probably going to start filming sometime next week. Do you think you will be free?"

"Yeah I should be but call me Monday. I'm actually on my way up to Boston for a little R&R."

"Ok no problem. Enjoy yourself and I'll call you on Monday."

Vinny was all up in Luca's business and was curious who was on the phone.

"Who was that?"

"Bianca did I tell you that Vinny is a jealous guy and needs to know everything I do? Vin what part of shut up and drive didn't you understand?"

"I just want to know who that was."

"Holy shit you're worst than a jealous girlfriend, it was my producer he called to tell me that we are starting production next week. Is that ok with you honey?"

"Oh ok. Luca you know I'm still against all this shit but you know me I'm just a jealous girlfriend."

Nikki couldn't help but laugh, "Are you guys always like this?"

"We are actually behaving today."

"This is like my own private comedy show, Vin you should hang out with us more often."

"I like her Luca don't let go of this one."

"I don't plan to Vin." He kissed Nikki and motions to Vinny to continue driving.

By the time Vinny pulled into the valet at the most amazing hotel in Boston, Luca and Nikki were passed out in the back seat. Vinny just smirked and shook his head, "sleeping beauty we are here, wake your ass up!" Luca and Nikki wake up and look around.

"Nice hotel."

"Only the best for you."

"Come on Luca you had this picked out already, you didn't even know I was coming."

"Bianca but do you know who I am? I call they bow at my feet and throw whoever is in my room out. You don't understand who I am yet?" Nikki couldn't help but laugh out loud. Vinny just shook his head and rolled his eyes.

"Ok your majesty get out of my car before I throw you out."

"Oh you don't talk to royalty like that."

"Oh please you slept and I'm cranky, so let's just go check in and see what Carlo wants."

"You're right Vin, let's go in. I just love Boston so whenever I come I always feel like royalty especially at this hotel. It's like *Cheers* where everyone knows your name."

As soon opportunity presented itself, Nikki texted Larry to let him know what Hotel they were staying in. She wasn't wired so she had to keep in touch with him. However, Luca and Vinny's phones were bugged. They entered the front door to go and check in and the hotel was definitely a five star establishment. Nikki was amazed how gorgeous just the lobby was: The beautiful Italian tiled floors, the chandeliers that were all crystal and just the atmosphere bespoke classy and rich. When they went to the front desk to check in the clerk told them that they needed to go to the fourth floor for a special check in. Nikki was very impressed. Luca looked at Vinny, "see I told you royalty." Vinny just rolled his eye. They got to the fourth floor and headed to the priority VIP check in. Vinny of course, had his own room. Nikki was a little taken back.

"I'm sorry I just assumed you two would be sharing and I would have my own."

"Why would I want to sleep with Vinny?"

"Because you are not sleeping with me, that's for sure."

"Ouch that hurt. Don't worry about it I could not let you sleep alone."

Vinny looked at them both, "Well I'm glad I'm alone, unless Bianca you want to share my room?"

She laughed because she knew Vinny was just trying to get a rise out of Luca. "I don't know Vinny, I might have to take you up on that offer because some people are just a little cocky and secure about themselves and that kind of turns me off a little."

Luca put his hand to his heart, "Oh you just continue to kill me softly. Come on I will make it all up to you once we get in the room."

Vinny interrupted, "Ah Luca, we need to meet with Mr. DeVito so come on enough of the small talk. Let's go put the bags down and go."

"You're right Vin, let's go check out our room and I'll meet you in fifteen minutes."

Luca and Nikki walked over to their suite. He opened the door and was very pleased. They had everything they needed in the room. The bed was set in the middle of the room with mirrors as a back board. There was a sitting area with a desk so one could work. There was a dining area that was already set up with champagne, strawberries and whip cream. Nikki thought to herself, *he certainly went above and beyond.* She was very impressed. Luca grabbed her from behind and kisses her neck,

"You like it?"

"It's amazing you really out did yourself and you shouldn't have done that."

"Why not? Anything for you."

"Well you really haven't known me that long and this is a little expensive, don't you think?"

"Babe there's no price tag on love."

"Love?" Did you just say LOVE?"

"Did I say that out loud?"

"Yeah Luca, you did." Nikki broke away from him and looked him in the face, "Luca how can you say that?"

"Bianca I don't know what you did to me but you did something and I can't help but feel this way for you. I know it's a short time but I have this strong connection with you and if it's love, then it's love. She didn't know how to respond so she just grabbed him and kissed him. They were so wrapped up in the kiss that they didn't hear the knock on the door.

Vinny was getting annoyed on the other side of it, "Oh come on already, you guys can do whatever you want after this meeting!"

Nikki pulled away and laughed, "Go before he huffs, puffs and blows the door down."

"Will you be ok while we are at this meeting?"

"Yes, I'm going to get my camera and walk over to the Public Garden. Meet me there when you guys are done and we can do lunch."

"Sounds like a plan, make sure you have your phone on you because I will be checking up on you."

"Oh really, I didn't know I was being watched?"

"My eyes are everywhere, I see everything you do."

"Yeah I doubt that, but if believing it makes your day better, then keep saying that to yourself."

He kissed her and walked out, "Oh Vin you need to get laid, you have way too much anger in you."

"Luca I'm a nervous wreck. I have no clue why they are sending me to meet with Carlo. Don't you find that strange?"

"Listen Vin, I'm here with you and I got your back. They are not going to do anything to you with me here, and anyway we told the boss I was coming. If something was up he would've made me stay home."

"What if they are going to whack us both?"

"Vin you forgot who I am? They will not whack me."

With that said Vinny calmed down and tried to get it out of his head. They pulled up to the biggest estate in Boston. The house was a mansion behind it Luca saw that they had horses, and right away he thought of the day he had with Nikki horseback riding. The garage was filled with the most expensive sports cars, a red Ferrari Testarossa, a black Lamborghini and of course a beautiful white Maserati. The property consisted of at least 4 acres of land. They had a tennis court, a basketball court and a volleyball court next to the pool. It was like being on a private resort with all the activities included. Luca just looked at Vinny.

"One day we will have this, I promise you my friend. Once my first movie comes out it's endless after that."

"Yeah if we make it out of here alive." Luca smacked Vinny in the back of his head, "will you snap out of it already?" They pulled up to the front of the gate and the security guard let them in. Carlo was waiting for Vinny and was surprised to see Luca with him.

"Luca what a nice surprise, I didn't know you were coming?"

"Yeah I love Boston so I never turn down an opportunity, plus I wanted to give Vinny some company. Is it a problem that I'm here?"

"No, not at all, I mean I'm glad to see you after four years but I had some stuff I wanted Vinny to bring back to New York; I can't risk you getting caught with it. That's why I asked for Vinny."

"Oh I see, well like I said I'm here for company and just to get some fresh air so if you and Vinny have business to take care of I can step out."

"No Luca you are here now so sit down have some coffee and let's talk."

Vinny finally calmed down, he knew that he wasn't going to get whacked, and all he was here to do was bring drugs back into New York without getting busted. The boys sat down and Carlo was explaining to them that they had a huge shipment from Canada and that they were going to bring some down for the New York families. He also explained to them that if they are happy with this new family from Canada, that next week they would be getting a bigger shipment. Luca was soaking this all in and he did not like it at all. He knew that once he became boss Carlo was not going to be his biggest fan. Carlo DeVito was the biggest drug lord and his whole business was about drugs. Luca thought to himself *this is why he's got this big house and all those cars. I will have that one day but I'm going to do it in a legitimate way. I am going to do it through the entertainment business.* Carlo took Vinny to the back and Luca didn't want to go, so he went to see the horses instead. Once Vinny was done they said their goodbyes.

"Luca it was really nice seeing you and I will see you this weekend at the party."

"Yes of course I will be there."

"Vinny I trust you with that and that you will make it to New York in one piece."

"Yes of course Carlo."

"Ok boys enjoy your stay here in Boston. Oh Luca I know you're a huge Yankee fan I have some tickets for tonight's game if you want to go."

"Oh that's nice of you. You just saved me a trip to the stadium to go get them. Thanks a lot Carlo I'll see you this weekend."

They got in the car and took off. Luca was just staring at Vinny,

"What Luca why are you staring at me?"

"Did you know that's what the meeting was about?"

"Of course not, I thought I was getting whacked!"

"So then what was all that in the back when you two took off and left the room?"

"He just wanted to show me something."

"Ok if you say so. Bianca said she would meet us at the Public Gardens, so let's go get her and grab some lunch before the game tonight."

"I don't know if I want to be the third wheel Luca."

"Listen you're my buddy as long as you don't come back in the room with us tonight, I'll be ok with you coming along."

"Fine, but none of that mushy kissing crap, because it kills me."

"Yeah buddy I'm sorry I can't promise that, you know I'm all about public affection and showing off what I have, and have you seen Bianca?"

When they got to the Gardens and found Bianca snapping some pictures and some guy standing next to her, talking to her. Luca was very particular about his stuff and the fact that some man is next to his woman made him flip out. He walked over and Nikki just turned around and smiled.

"I thought you dumped me here and were never coming back."

"Is that why you are talking to this man?" Nikki's smile changed into an angry scowl. *Who is he to tell me who I can talk to?* Vinny saw where this was going so he motioned to the guy to take a hike and walk away now.

"I'm sorry, what are you saying to me Luca, that I'm not allowed to talk to anyone of the opposite sex?"

"Babe you're my woman and it has to stay that way."

"Luca BABE you need to relax yourself, and you need to know that I have a lot of male friends. I am not a possession so don't treat me like one."

"WOW Luca, I really like her."

Luca realized that he did step out of line, and he didn't want to ruin the two days away with her, so he hugged her and apologized. Nikki thought it was cute that he got all jealous but she did have a lot of male friends and he couldn't flip out every time someone spoke to her. He agreed and they all went out to lunch. They all had a good time. After lunch they all went back to the room to get ready for the Yankee and Soxs game. Nikki was very excited she was a huge Yankee fan, Derek Jeter was her favorite. They didn't have much time so she threw on her Jersey with a pair Jeans. Luca loved the way she looked. She grabbed her Yankee hat and put her hair up.

Luca grabbed her and kissed her, "as anyone told you how hot you are?"

She laughed, "Come on Jeter is waiting."

Luca tried to hide his feelings but it was really tough. He was the jealous type and he really didn't like that comment. Vinny was downstairs waiting. They got into the car and left. Vinny looked at Nikki and she had Yankees on from head to toe,

"Ah Bianca you realize we are in Boston and they hate Yankee fans?"

"Yes I know."

"But you have Yankees on from top to bottom."

"Yes, I know that too." Luca was just waiting and laughing he knew she was going to come out with some kid of sarcastic remark.

"Well you know they are going to kill us?"

"Really Vinny I thought you were a tough guy? No one is going to mess with the two of you. Are you actually scared?"

Luca laughed. "And there it is. I was waiting for you to say something."

"Great you did this on purpose to prove a point?"

"And what point is that my new friend?"

"You just want us to get killed!"

"Oh Vinny don't worry, I have a black belt. I'll protect you from the big bad Boston fans."

"Yeah, yeah make fun, you will see once we walk in the stadium."

They got to the stadium and showed the usher the tickets. They were right behind the Yankee dugout. Nikki was very excited she was never this close to Jeter. Jeter was up stretching and Nikki was just looking at him.

Then Vinny and his big mouth screamed, "Yo Jeter! The lady here wants to take a picture with you." Luca gave Vinny a nasty look and Nikki got all embarrassed.

Jeter looked at Nikki and smiled, "Sure come here and take a picture." Nikki was so excited she couldn't believe Jeter was going to take a picture with her but she acted calm, cool and collected. Luca on the other hand wanted to put a bullet in Vinny's head. He knew how hot Nikki was, and Jeter would be in his glory to have his arm around her waist. Vinny knew he fucked up and that Luca was going to fuck him up but, he helped Nikki down to the dugout so she could take her picture.

Nikki gave Luca the camera, he thought, *great not only do I have to watch this I got to tell the stupid fuck to smile too.* Jeter grabbed her hand and said hello. Nikki introduced herself as Bianca Monteleone.

"Bianca, that's a really nice name."

"Thank you."

They looked at Luca; Jeter had his arm around her waist and their faces were cheek to cheek. Luca's blood was boiling but he felt confident because he knew that Nikki was going home with him and not Jeter. He gave her kiss on the cheek and an autograph. She thanked him and wished him luck. She went back to sit with Luca and Vinny.

"Wow that was exciting, thanks Vinny."

"I have to hand it to you Bianca you were nice and calm, and didn't get all star struck."

"Thanks, I didn't want to make an ass out of myself."

"Yeah thanks for that Vin." Vinny knew that Luca was being sarcastic.

They sat and watch the game and it was an intense one. Vinny was right all the fans were getting nasty with Nikki because she was a Yankee fan. She ignored them but the boys were getting pissed. They weren't used to just sitting there taking the abuse, but Nikki told them to just back off and let them vent. The Yankees were behind they were losing five to two, it was the bottom of the ninth and the Yankees were up. The fans behind Nikki were taunting her saying how they were going to lose big because the Red Soxs are the best. She was calm, bases were loaded and Jeter was up. She turned to the fans behind her

"My boy is up and that he is going to wipe that grin off your faces." They laughed.

"Yeah he needs a grand slam."

She turned over to Jeter and yelled out to him. "Jeter GRAND SLAM! I KNOW YOU CAN DO IT!"

He smiled and tipped his hat. On the second swing Jeter hit it out of the park. Vinny, Luca and the fans behind Nikki just stood there dumb founded. Their jaws dropped. "How the fuck did you do that?"

Nikki just stood there yelling, "YEAH JETER!"

Jeter touched home plate spoke to the Ref and took the game winning ball. He signed it and walked over to Nikki. "Thank you, you seem to be a good luck charm." He handed her the ball and kissed her on the cheek. She turned beat red.

Luca looked at him, "Jeter that's already one too many kisses tonight."

He laughed and said goodbye and walked away. Nikki looked at Luca,

"What did I tell you about that?"

"Talking is one thing but when I see a man kissing you then that's a different story."

"Ok just this time I will let it go, but come on it's Jeter; he's got models falling all over him."

"Babe have you looked in the mirror?"

"Oh please you are just being nice."

Vinny looked around and noticed the fans getting really loud towards them. "Ah guys, can we take this back to the hotel? The crowd seems to be going nuts."

Nikki stopped and looked around, "WOW Boston fans really do hate us." She laughed grabbed Luca's hand and all three walked out to the car.

Luca offered for them to go out to dinner but Vinny was tired and they were heading back to New York tomorrow. Nikki said she just wanted to go back to the room because she had a long day.

Luca loved that idea. "Sounds like a plan we can order some room service and just hang out." She smiled and excused herself. She had to touch base with Larry and George. Luca was waiting for her back in the room, he ordered sushi for them.

"What took you so long?"

"I stopped by the gift shop but it was closed."

"I ordered us some sushi. I hope its ok that I ordered for you."

"Yes of course I'm a big fan of sushi now, but if you don't mind I would like to take a shower first."

Luca put his arms around her waist, "Can I come in with you?"

"No! I don't think I'm ready for that yet."

"Fine, be like that, but I'm sure if Jeter was here you would say yes to him."

"Well if Jeter was here that would be a different story." She knew that would piss him off and she was teasing him.

"WOW that's really a low blow."

Nikki kissed him and went to take a shower.

She took a nice long hot shower. When she got out she realized she hadn't taken any clothes into the bathroom with her, and she had to walk out with a towel. She knew Luca was going to be all over her but it was a chance she had to take. She opened the door and Luca was watching TV waiting for her to come and eat. Before he looked up to see her he said, "The sushi came while you were in the shower." Then he turned around and realized she was standing there in a towel and her long wet hair. Her legs were so long just the thought of them wrapped around him was turning him on.

"What are you doing to me?"

"I'm sorry I forgot to bring my clothes in the bathroom."

"Don't be sorry, you are amazing." He grabbed her and started to kiss her.

"Luca I don't think this is a good idea." He continued to kiss her and ignored what she was saying. "I don't know if I'm ready for this." Nikki loved every minute and she knew she wanted it just as bad. It was just wrong because this was work and she was falling for him. She was so confused and didn't know what to do. Luca grabbed her hair and continued to kiss her neck. Nikki was fighting it but she knew she wanted him. "Luca really, I think maybe—"

Luca put his finger on her lips. "Shhhh Just let it go and enjoy it." With that said he started to kiss her, pulling her closer. He sat on the bed and she was still standing. He looked up at her pulled away her hair, "what did you do to me?" She straddled him and pushed him down on the bed. He took her towel off and he just admired her beauty. "You are so beautiful."

Nikki smiled took off his shirt, "you're not so bad yourself." She started to kiss him, her long hair falling all around him. He had her by her hips. She pulled up again and he put his hand on her neck and worked his way down to her chest. She unbuttoned his pants and smiled.

"You are a bad girl you."

She continued to smile and he helped her take his pants off. They started again and she was still on top of him. He held her so tight and pulled her hair back kissing her neck and working his way down to her breasts. She started to lose control. He flipped her on her back and gave her a big bite on her neck. He continued to kiss her. He got to her breasts and just caressed them, with his tongue he started to play with her nipple. She loved his touch and the way her body tingled with every move of his tongue. She grabbed the sheets with both of her hands and let out a moan. She couldn't resist him. She grabbed him and flipped him on his back. "Impressive, I love a woman who likes to take control." She just smiled and started to suck on his neck. Luca loved it, "FUCK," he grabbed her by her hair and kissed her. He cupped her face in his big hands and just looked straight into her eyes, "You are driving me crazy." She smiled and went back down to his neck licking him and working her way down to his inner thigh and teased him. "Fuck Bianca you are killing me." She smiled and gave in to his desire. He just looked down at her threw his head back letting out pleasurable moans. He was losing control, "I want to make love to you." She looked up with her hair falling around her face, "Oh you haven't seen anything yet!" She proceeded to get on top of him. Next thing you know he was inside her and they started to make love. She was in control and he loved it. Luca grabbed her hips and pulled her down more pushing himself inside deeper into her. She leaned back; he touched her and continued to make love to her. He turned her around, this really turned him on because there was a mirror for a backboard and he enjoyed watching her while making love to her. He pulled her hair back and just continued to make love to her from behind. They were both ready to reach their climax and Nikki made sure to let him know. He loved to hear that. They both got satisfied and just dropped on the bed.

He held her so tight, "I don't know what you did to me but I think you just made it worse."

"I know I never felt like this before and I shouldn't be doing this."

"You were amazing."

"So were you. You know exactly how to do me."

They just held each other for a while. Luca started to get hungry and almost forgot that the sushi was there already. "Come on let's eat some sushi, we need our energy."

Nikki threw on a robe and they sat and fed each other sushi. She didn't feel that she was on an assignment; this was just too surreal for her. She was falling for this man and that was wrong in every way. They ate and drank and started to learn more about each. They made love at least three more times before they actually passed out and went to bed.

* * * * *

VINNY CALLED THEM EARLY the next morning so they could start on their way back to New York. Luca and Nikki had had a long night, but they got up. He told Vinny to meet him on the fourth floor and they would have breakfast before they left.

Luca looked at Nikki, "Good morning Babe how did you sleep?"

"Great."

"I can see by the smile you have from ear to ear."

"Oh no! Is it that obvious?"

"How about we make up some time and take a shower together?"

She smiled and went into the bathroom giving him the eye as to welcome him into the shower with her. He smiled, "You don't have to twist my arm." They made love in the shower but they didn't save any time, they took longer. Poor Vinny remained in the dining room patiently waiting for the two love birds to come out, so they could eat and leave. They finally made it out of their room and found Vinny sitting and eating. Nikki was amazed at the set up of the dining room. There was a sitting area with love seats and couches in front of a fire place. Little tables set to the side so one could sit and have breakfast. On the other side was another dining area with tables set up so you can play chess. That room also had couches and love seats. Nikki felt like she was first class and thought to herself *I can live like this* but then snapped herself back into to reality when she saw a text from Larry. He asked her how her night went and if she was ok. She texted back that she was fine and that they were heading back today. Luca got her some breakfast and told her to eat; she needed energy after last night. Vinny just rolled his eyes,

"Is that what I heard last night? You guys were loud!" Nikki's face dropped. Vinny laughed

"I'm just kidding but now I know what you guys did last night."

Luca slapped him on the back of his head. "When are you going to grow up and act like a gentleman? She's a classy lady and I never want to hear you talk about her like that again." Vinny felt bad and apologized. They finished breakfast got their bags and headed to the car.

CHAPTER 15

Luca DECIDED HE WAS going to drive. Vinny sat on the passenger side and Nikki sat in the back. She was exhausted and she wanted to take a nap. The ride to New York was pretty quiet. They had been driving for two hours when Luca realized there were cops behind him. He hit Vinny on his arm, "Oh there are cops behind us."

Vinny had fallen asleep too and woke up and looked towards the back. "Ok so don't worry, it's not like they have their lights on." Just as he said that the lights went on and singled them to pull over. Vinny now got very nervous. "Luca we can't stop."

Luca just looked at Vinny, "why it's not like we are doing anything wrong." By this time Nikki also woke up and looked back to see what was going on. "No Luca really we can't stop." Luca just gave Vinny a dirty look and continued to drive.

"Why Vin, what the fuck are you not telling me?"

"Listen man, I'm loaded."

"WHAT THE FUCK DO YOU MEAN?"

"Well Carlo gave me the stuff to bring back and I have it on me." Luca was livid, he flipped out. Nikki was in the back and she realized what was going on. Vinny had drugs on him and if they got pulled over the whole case could go to shit.

"YOU STUPID SON OF A BITCH! What the fuck is wrong with you? How dare you do that shit behind my back?"

"Luca what the fuck was I supposed to do?"

"That's why you walked out with Carlo so he can give you the stuff?"

"Lu I couldn't have said no."

"I swear to God Vin you know how much I hate that shit, but to do it behind my back and now you put Bianca at risk? WHAT THE FUCK WERE YOU THINKING?"

"Lu you need to calm down."

"CALM DOWN? CALM DOWN?" Luca took out his gun and pointed it to Vinny's head. "YOU STUPID SON OF A BITCH, I SHOULD SHOOT YOU RIGHT NOW!"

"Luca it's me Vinny, your buddy don't be stupid."

"The only stupid person in this car is you."

"Luca I'm sorry but you need to just stop and think and put the gun away." Nikki was getting nervous she never saw this side of Luca before. He totally flipped out on Vinny. Luca stopped and thought for a minute.

"Ok asshole take the fucking gun, you know what you have to do, RIGHT?"

"Yeah I do."

Luca finally pulled over. The officer got out of the squad car and advanced towards them, gun drawn. Vinny got out with his hands up, he slammed the car door and Luca just took off at full speed. The officer seeing Luca take off, ran back in his car and started to chase after him. Nikki was pissed, she wondered *what the fuck is going on here?* Vinny was left on the side of the road with no car and nowhere to go. He had to walk to the next exit and jump on a train. Luca was just driving full speed with the cops were still on his tail as he now had at least three police cars chasing him. "These fucking assholes think they can catch me." He kept looking back at Nikki, "babe, are you ok?"

She kept looking back at the cops, "I think so. What the fuck is going on?" Luca was just trying to pay attention to the road, "Vinny is an asshole." Nikki sent Larry a text explaining what was going on. She wrote to him, "get these fucking pigs off our tail or the whole case will go to hell!!." She was pissed.

Larry texted back, "Look at you talking all gangster, I think you have been hanging out with them too long."

Nikki was not in a joking mood, "Larry, get them off my fucking tail NOW!" She kept looking back to see if they were backing off. Finally she realized that they turned off the road and they lost them. She finally relaxed.

Luca looked back and realized that he lost the cops. "Did I tell you that I'm related to Mario Andretti?

Nikki laughed to herself because she knew that Larry was the one who called it in. She was pissed, they went to get drugs and the chief had to know about this. They have tabs all over DeVito, she wondered *"why didn't he tell me?"* She intended to pay the chief a visit today when she got back. Nikki was just looking out the window. Luca saw that she was in deep thought.

"Bianca, what's the matter?" She was taken by surprise. She couldn't tell him that she was thinking about his case, and what the chief could possibly be hiding.

"I'm just thinking of poor Vinny. Why did you leave him on the side of the road and how is he getting back? Shouldn't we be turning around and going to get him?"

"I know you're not stupid and I know you pretty much have an idea what line of work I'm in. You see Vinny had drugs on him."

"Yeah that much I got."

"Well we always put them on us because if we get pulled over the car takes off, making the cops thinks that the drugs are in the car but in the meantime it's with the guy who is left stranded on the side of the road."

Nikki thought about it and understood, *that's why they never find anything in the cars.* She found that to be really good information. So next time they would just grab the guy on the side of road.

"Ok so then, explain something else to me."

"What's that?"

"Why did you get all crazy on Vinny? I never seen that side of you, than again I don't know you that long, but that freaked me out a little."

"Vinny didn't think, he put you at risk. If God forbid we would've gotten stopped than they would've taken you in too and I couldn't live with that. He knows very well that I hate the drugs and that I plan to make our money the legitimate way. He didn't tell me because I would've told him to go home alone and that would have pissed him off. So you see, he ends up alone."

"So how will he get home?"

"He will take a train."

"So this isn't the first time?"

"No not at all. Babe, let's forget about Vinny, tell me what did you think about the last two days?"

"I really had a good time, thank you for thinking of me and taking me along."

"The pleasure was all mine. What are your plans later?"

"Actually when I get back I have to stop by the office and then probably just relax at home. Tomorrow is the big party."

"Yes, that's right. How about I pick up some groceries, some wine and come over and make you dinner?"

"Really, you want to cook for me?"

"Yes, I will make you an off the hook dinner."

"Ok well let's see how the day goes."

They arrived at Nikki's place. Luca told her that he will see her around six. Nikki thought that gave her enough time to go see the chief. She kissed him goodbye and he left. The minute she got into her apartment and closed the door behind her, she called Larry.

"Larry what the fuck happened at that meeting? I know that DeVito is bugged so what do we have?"

"He is bugged but it's not our guy Nikki, we don't work that family."

"What are you talking about?"

"Well apparently Mike is on the DeVito's."

"Really, I thought I was on this ALONE?" Nikki was pissed! She knew something smelled fishy and if she had her way Mike would be sleeping with the fishes! She stopped and thought, *I am hanging out with them too much I'm starting to talk like them too much.*

"I guess not Nikki. So how was your get away?" Nikki blushed she couldn't tell Larry that she slept with Luca.

"Well the best thing was I got to meet Jeter and take a picture with him."

"WOW that's great!"

"Listen I need to meet with the chief and I really don't need to be followed, so just keep an ear out and if anything call me."

"Ok, but why are you going in? The chief specifically said to stay away."

"Yeah, that's why I'm going."

"I don't get it."

"I'll explain once I know what's going on."

"Ok, just watch yourself Nikki."

"I always do."

She hung with Larry and jumped in the shower. She got dressed and headed to the office. She was so pissed.

She felt betrayed and lied to. She kept thinking maybe he didn't know or it slipped their mind but she was just kidding herself. When Nikki arrived she found Mike inside with the chief. Mike looked pretty pissed himself. He had his hands up screaming and yelling, and what got Nikki wondering was that the chief had his head down like he was the one who did something wrong. She looked around and saw Greg, "What's going on in there?"

"I don't know. Mike is pissed about something going wrong."

Nikki knew something was not right. The Chief looked up and did a double take when he saw Nikki. Mike turned around and looked more pissed than before. He opened the door

"What are you doing here?"

"I work here asshole, what's your excuse?"

"Oh the comedian is back."

"What's your problem Mikey, didn't get laid in a few centuries?"

"Oh yeah you didn't say that last night when I was banging you."

"In your dreams!" The chief screamed from his office, "ENOUGH, BOTH OF YOU! Nikki what are you doing here I thought I told you to stay away until the case was done? Something happened in Boston?" Nikki walked into his office.

"Why don't you tell me Chief?"

"What are you talking about Nikki?"

"You knew they were going there because Carlo DeVito had received a shipment. You knew they were going to bring drugs back. Why didn't you tell me? Did you also have the cops chase us? Do you want to see me mess up on this case?"

"Nikki we really didn't know that Carlo was going to have Vinny bring back drugs. We had an idea about the shipment but we didn't have any hard evidence. We are waiting for something bigger."

'FOR WHAT?"

"Nikki you are out of line."

"I'm sorry Chief but when I heard that Mike is involved in this case too it pissed me off!"

"Who told you that?"

"It doesn't matter. I just thought it was just me."

"Well Mike is doing something different so the case is still all you. You need to just keep your eyes opened and be careful and DO NOT come back to the office, it's just too risky."

"Fine! But DO NOT keep anything from me either."

Nikki walked out of the office and didn't even look at anyone. The chief just looked at Mike and shook his head. Mike wasn't too pleased with Nikki. He found her to be too annoying and way too nosey! She called Larry to give him an update and went straight home.

*   *   *   *   *

WHEN LUCA ARRIVED HOME, HE found Vinny waiting for him outside. Luca was still very mad at him. He walked past him and headed upstairs.

"Are you kidding me? I had to walk I don't know how many miles to the nearest exit and then find a train station so I can get home, and you walk past me like I don't exist?"

"Vin you are lucky I don't beat the fuck out of you right now. I don't know even know why you are here, aren't you afraid for your life?"

"No actually you have my car and I just want it back."

"Yeah well after what you pulled today I'm taking the car. Yeah that's what I'm doing, I'm going to take your car."

"You can't do that!"

"You seem to keep forgetting who I am. I can do whatever I want."

They walked into the apartment and Luca threw his bag on the floor. He turned around and saw Vinny that was still behind him, "you still here?"

Vinny put his hand out, "Give me the keys."

Luca turned his face because he knew he would laugh, "No the car is mine, go fuck yourself."

Vinny was still standing there, "my keys please."

Luca laughed and threw them at him, "here, because you look like you're going to cry." They sat on the couch and Vinny turns to Luca,

"By the way thanks for coming to Boston with me, even though you tried to kill me."

"Yeah, even though you're a stupid fuck, I will always have your back. What did you do with the stuff?"

"I have to bring it to the boss."

"WHAT?"

"I have to bring it to the boss, why?"

"YOU STILL HAVE IT ON YOU?"

"Yeah Lu, I just got back you had my car what the fuck do I look like, superman with a cape that I can fly from place to place?"

"Vin, get your car, get your drugs and get the fuck out of my place."

"Holy Shit Lu, but you are crazy with this shit."

"Asshole, I just came out. The last thing I want is to go back in, so do me a favor, go!"

"Okay, okay. What are you doing later?"

"I'm going to Bianca's. I'm going to make her the best dinner she ever had."

"You never made me dinner."

"Yeah, well you don't have gorgeous green eyes, long legs, and long beautiful golden brown hair."

"And I'm sure having a dick doesn't help either."

"GET OUT YOU PIG! I swear you turned gay on me."

Vinny left and Luca took a quick shower. He went to the grocery store to pick up a few things for dinner. He knew exactly what he was going to make her his famous pasta with shrimps and Broccolini. He grabbed all the ingredients. Broccoli Rabe, Broccolini, one pound of shrimps deveined and cleaned, beef bouillon and of course some garlic. He was looking forward to seeing her. He had just dropped her off a few hours ago but he was missing her so much, and couldn't understand what she did to him to make him like this. He couldn't remember ever feeling like that. He paid for the groceries and went to the Liquor store to pick up some Moscato. He knew it was her favorite.

* * * * *

NIKKI GOT REALLY EXCITED when she heard the knock on the door. She tried to control herself and didn't want to look too eager so she waited for him to knock again. She finally let him in.

"What took you so long?"

"I had to get rid of the other guy in my room."

"WHAT?"

"Oh my God, I'm just teasing."

"Babe that's not even funny." Nikki helped him with the bags and put them on the counter.

"So what are you making for dinner?"

"I'm a master chef, whatever I make is going to make your taste buds dance."

"Ok, so tell me what you need and if I can help."

"Open the wine and just watch me cook. I want you to just relax and enjoy me."

"Have I mentioned how cocky you are?"

"Yes, thank you, I love when you compliment me."

She just shook her head and watched Luca start cooking. He started with two cups of water and put the Broccolini and Broccoli in the pot. He crushed five cloves of garlic and added them to the pot. He let that boil for about fifteen minutes and then added the pound of shrimps and the beef bouillon. In the mean time he strained the Pasta. He added everything together and let it cook for an extra five minutes. He turned around and smiled at Nikki who was already on her second glass of wine. "That was fast." He grabbed the glass and took a sip, "it's only twenty minutes." She had already set the table and he dished the pasta and put it on the table. He looked at her and dared her to try it.

She was amazed she really liked it. "I am very impressed Luca, this is really good."

Luca smiled and took a sip of wine. "Did you actually think it was going to be bad?" Nikki rolled her eyes at his cockiness,

"I was afraid you were going to burn my kitchen down but I was wrong. I guess you will be making dinner from this point on."

"As long as you are dessert I will be your own personal chef."

"I think we have a deal." They finished eating. Nikki got up to clean up and Luca helped her. She started to wash the dishes and he came right behind her. He put his arms around her and started to kiss her neck.

"Luca it's a little hard washing the dishes like this."

He turned her around, turned the water off and continued to kiss her. Nikki was in his thrall and couldn't stop herself. Luca picked her up and placed her on the kitchen island. She wrapped her long legs around him and whispered in his ear, "I hope you like your dessert HOT because I'm on fire." He laughed and just continued to kiss her. She took her top off and he just admired her. He picked her up again and put her on the couch. He took his shirt off and she admired him. He got on top of her. She wrapped her legs around him. They were both enjoying each other. He picked her up again and this time they went into the bedroom. She laughed, "I see we are leaving a trail of clothes in every room." He got her on the bed and removed her pants. She returned the favor by removing his and getting on top of him. She loved to be in control and he loved a woman who was in control. She loved the way he made her feel. They made love all night. They fell asleep in each other arms. Nikki woke up screaming "LUCA" again. She had the dream that she had been having every night.

Luca, startled, jumped out of bed, "Babe I'm right here, what's wrong?"

"I'm sorry I didn't mean to wake you up. I just keep having the same nightmare every night and each night something else is added to the dream."

"Babe if you're dreaming of me it's not a nightmare."

"You're funny but I'm serious Luca, it's not a good dream and I don't know what it means."

"Well why don't you tell me and maybe we can figure it out together, heck I'm in it I think I should know what you're dreaming about."

"You're sweet but it's ok, it's just a dream." She looked down and Luca sensed that this dream was really bothering her.

He lifted her chin up, "I'm serious I know it's bothering you please tell me."

She rolled her eyes and she explained to him how she's in the car driving in the pouring rain, and the only thing on her mind is to get to Luca. She continued by saying, "I know you are in danger because I sense it. I get by the train tracks and the bar comes down because a train is coming. I come out and it's pouring but tonight in my dream, I heard a gunshot."

She looked sad and Luca just grabbed her face with his big hands and just kissed her, "it's just a dream, I'm here and I'm not going anywhere, I promise."

Nikki smiled and they just hugged. He grabs her face again, "what did I ever do to deserve you?" She blushed and looked away, "I'm not all that, stop saying that."

He turned her face around, "are you kidding me? You are the best thing that ever happened to me, I love you Bianca."

She noticed the sincerity in his face, "I love you too Luca." They kissed and made love again.

The next morning Nikki woke up with a big smile on her face and realized how hungry she felt. She laughed to herself, "It has to be all that sex last night that made me so hungry." She turned to look and Luca was gone. She frowned but that quickly turned into a bigger smile when, she smelled bacon, eggs and coffee. "Is he making breakfast?" She threw on her robe and went to the kitchen. She found Luca behind the stove making breakfast.

He turned and smiled, "Good Morning Babe. I didn't want to wake you, you look so peaceful and after that nightmare, I wanted to let you sleep." She walked behind him put her arms around his waist, he thought he was going to get a kiss but she grabbed a piece of bacon instead and walked away. "Oh! I get up early, I make you sleep longer, I even make you breakfast and you can't give me a morning kiss?"

Nikki laughed and went back over to him, put her arms around him and nibbled on his ear, whispering, "Oh I can give you more than just a kiss."

Luca's eyes widened and he turned around and grabbed her, giving her the biggest kiss as he picked her up. He turned to turn off the stove, then put her on the breakfast nook. "Oh I know what I want for breakfast." She smiled and just pulled him closer and they made love right the in the kitchen.

Much later they sat down and had breakfast. She noticed he had something on his mind.

"What's wrong?"

"Nothing, just thinking about tonight and the big party."

"Oh that's right, is that tonight?"

"Yeah, why you say it like that?"

"Oh I meant to tell you, I can't make it, I have other plans."

"Yeah, ok the only plans you have is to be by my side so I can show you off."

"Oh is that what you are going to do, show me off? Well in that case I will be there, but all joking aside, I do have a day of beauty planned so you can show me off."

"You are perfect just the way you are."

"Oh you are so sweet, but really I need to go do my nails, hair and all that girlie stuff we do."

Luca laughed, "Ok, ok, I get it. I actually have some stuff to do before tonight. So you get all dolled up and I will pick you up around six."

"Sounds good to me."

Luca got up kissed Nikki and went to take a shower. Once he was done, he left and promised to pick her up later. The minute he left Nikki called Larry to make sure everything was set for tonight. She was very excited that she was going in from the inside, but at the same time she was so confused about her feelings for Luca. She had grown so close to him and she really and truly started to feel love for him. She shook the feeling off and went off to her spa day.

CHAPTER 16

NIKKI WAS PUTTING THE finishes touches on her make up when she heard a knock on the door. She got butterflies in her stomach; she felt like a school girl getting ready for the prom. She was nervous and excited at the same time. She walked over and opened the door. Luca just stood there in amazement. Nikki looked gorgeous she had on the red Dolce & Gabana dress that he bought her. She was tall and slender so it fit her perfectly. She was fit so her arms had some nice definition. Her hair wasn't fully up but it was softly pinned up and her long locks of curls came down her back. She wasn't one to wear a lot of makeup her face was naturally made up. She looked like she came out of Glamour Magazine. Luca was speechless, "Babe! Oh my God you look absolutely stunning!"

Nikki didn't take compliments too well and blushed, "Oh please, I look horrible."

Luca did a double take, "what are you smoking, have you looked in the mirror?" She smiled, "yes I have and I look ok."

Luca grabbed her by the waist, "If we didn't have to leave for this party, I would fuck the shit out of you right now!"

She pulled back and thought about what he said, "Luca!"

He just laughed, "What you don't like talking dirty?"

She gave him a grin, "No, because I was just thinking the same thing about you!" They both laughed.

She spun around and he couldn't take his eyes off of her, "you know there will be a lot of jealous people there tonight."

She grabbed both of his hands and admired how he looked, "You know I can see why, you look hot Luca!"

"There's no question how hot I look but when they see us both walk in, they are going to think, "WOW! Look at that power couple."

"You really are one cocky human being."

"I have to be, that's what makes me who I am. Listen, we need to go so grab your bag and let's get moving." Nikki grabbed everything and asked Luca if she should bring a shawl, just in case it would be cold. Luca looked at her with a devious smile, "I will be right there next to you keeping you hot all night!" She grabbed her shawl anyway and locked the door.

They pulled up to the Buoncuore Estate and Nikki searched and saw that her men where there. She was a little nervous but ready for the night. They pulled up to the gate and Luca announced himself, just as the gates were opening Luca looked at Nikki, "Babe wave for the feds, I want them to see what a gorgeous human being you are."

Nikki did a double take, for a minute she thought he figured her out. With a nervous shaking voice she responded to Luca, "what are you talking about, what feds?"

Luca raised his eyebrows, "Relax the feds are always around during these big parties. They actually think that we are stupid enough to do something, knowing they are all outside in marked cars."

Nikki thought about that it and said to herself, we are dumb for thinking that. She just gave Luca a nervous smile. They pulled up to the front and the valet went to open the door for Nikki but Luca beat him to it. He walked over and opened the door, grabbed Nikki by the hand and as she came out, all eyes were on Nikki.

Vinny who was talking to a few guys, stopped dead in his tracks, "is that Luca and Bianca?"

Nikki was very nervous at this point, "Luca what is everyone looking at?" Luca looks at her and just shakes his head, "Babe but do you think I'm kidding when I say you're hot?" As they walked in the main dining everyone looked and started to clap. Luca walked in proud with Nikki on his arm. He started to work the room and thanked everyone. Kisses and hugs from the family, welcoming him home. He felt like a King, introducing Nikki to everyone. He finally made his way to Mr. Buoncuore, stopped in front of him and they hugged.

"Luca my boy welcome."

"Thank you Mr. B, this is really some party."

"It's all for you my boy, all for you. Now why don't you introduce me to this beauty that you have next to you. Who is this beautiful woman?"

Luca looked over at his girl and smiled like the proud man he was. "This Mr. B. is the one and only Bianca Monteleone." He looked over at Nikki, "Bianca this is

Mr. Buoncuore." Nikki stuck her hand out to shake his hand but Mr. B just hugged and kissed her. Luca laughed, "Bianca, we don't shake hands in this family, we hug."

She smiled back at him, "Yeah, I noticed." Mr. Buoncuore grabbed a waiter and gave Luca and Bianca a glass of Dom Perignon. He hit his fork on the glass to get everyone's attention. When Mr. B talked, everyone listened. Everyone became really quiet and waited for the Boss to talk. He raised his glass and started to make a speech in Luca's honour.

"First of all, I would like to thank all the families for coming tonight to our little get together. Tonight we are here to celebrate a man of honor, loyalty, respect and sincerity. A man that everyone should use as an example of what we should be like. A man that did something that no one would do; he protected me and my family. A man that I can consider to be my son who would put his life on the line for what he believes in. This man is standing next to me tonight and I've always considered him my right hand guy, Luca! We are all very happy that you made it out and I speak for everyone when I say we are grateful to you." All the families started to clap and cheer. Vinny of course whistled and cheered the loudest. He was so proud of his best friend, that he actually had a tear in his eye.

Luca stepped up and raised his hands to quite the crowd. "Thank you Mr. B and thank all of you, I certainly feel the love. I want to start out by saying that I am honored and privileged to be part of this family and I know that if I had to do it all over again, I would.

Mr. B put his arm around Luca, "with that said let's all raise our glasses and welcome home Luca, Salute!" Mr. B whispered in Luca's ear that they were going to his office to discuss some business with the rest of the families and that he and Vinny should come. Luca nodded and told Nikki that he would be right back.

Nikki knew this could take some time so she told Luca she was just going over to the bar to get a drink. He nodded and she walked away but he kept his eye on her. He knew there were vultures in the room looking to prey on her and that they didn't give a shit with who she came with. As she walked over to the bar she was floored! Nikki couldn't believe who was standing by the bar. It was the two goons that hung out with Mike. She was SO pissed. She thought, *how can they send someone to watch me, and how the fuck are they involved?* She needed to get to Larry but she knew that wasn't possible. She walked over and ordered Vodka with Cranberry.

The goons looked over at her, then Joe looked at Paul, "She cleans up really well doesn't she Paul?"

Under her breath she warns them, "You ruin this, I will fuck you both up that you wish you were never born."

Joe looks at Paul and smirked, "she's still very feisty, isn't she?" Nikki turned towards them and smiled knowing that Luca was probably staring at her she had to act like nothing was going on.

"What are you two idiots doing here?"

"We are working, just like you."

"Really, how come I had no idea?"

Paul got close to her and whispered in her ear, "bitch you are NOT all that!"

Luca noticed this and his blood started to boil. He looked at Vinny with an angry look, "who are those two fucking idiots near my woman?"

Vinny glanced over and saw Paulie and Joey in Nikki's face. "Oh those are the new guys from Canada that I was telling you about."

Luca started to walk over to them, and Vinny knowing that Luca would probably flip out and make a scene, followed him. Luca realized all night that everyone was giving these guys too much attention. He was actually a little jealous. He thought to himself, *tonight is my night, why are these guys getting all the attention.* Nikki realized Luca coming towards them, warns Joe and Paul to step back and act normal. The boys stepped back and smiled like nothing was going on.

Luca walked over and put his arms on both of their shoulders. "Hello boys, I don't think we were formally introduced."

Vinny interrupted and introduced them. "Luca, this is Paul and Joey, the guys from Canada that we've been dealing with, boys, this is Luca." The boys shake his hand.

Luca still very pissed, "Well it's nice to finally put the faces with the voices."

The boys look at Luca, "It's very nice to meet you too."

"Now boys have you met MY Bianca?" Paul looks over at Nikki and smiled, "yes we just met." Joey looked over, "yes, Bianca it's very nice to meet you."

"She's gorgeous isn't she?" They both nod. "Well, if I ever see you talk to her again the way I saw you do before, I will hunt you down and kill you myself. Now from what I understand you wanted to talk to me about something that's coming?"

Joey fixed his jacket, "Yes if we can walk to the next room maybe we can go over some of the details."

Luca looked over at Nikki, "Will you be Ok here?"

She laughed, "I can take care of myself, plus I need to make a phone call so I will be by the garden when you are done."

He nodded and kissed her, then walked away with the two goons.

Nikki walked out into the garden and smiled at everyone she passed. She went to the gazebo and sat down. She couldn't call Larry, for fear that someone had ears so she texted him instead. She wanted to know why the goons were here, and why no one told her. Larry was just as confused as her and promised to look into it. She was pissed as she sat there just trying to make sense of everything. She looked up from her phone and he was standing there, just staring at her and smiling.

* * * * *

LUCA, VINNY AND THE goons went to the office where the rest of bosses were waiting for the big announcement from Mr. B. They walked in and Mr. Buoncuore motioned for the boys to have a seat. "As you all know I called you all back here to tell you that I decided to step down. Due to some medical issues, I have to take it easy. Therefore I decided that it was time for me to name my successor. We all know that Luca has been more like a son to me than anyone else. He has been there for me and the family and has taken one for the team." Everyone looked at Luca and smiled with approval and appreciation. "With that said, I would like to announce that I decided that Luca will take my place as of tonight." Everyone smiled with approval. They knew that Luca was the perfect man for the job. "Luca my boy come here." Luca got up and stood next to Mr. Buoncuore. "Luca you are the son I never had and I know I am making the right decision, I trust that you will lead the families in the right directions and make good decisions and of course if you need any advice, I'm here for you." He hugged Luca and kissed him Italian style, on both cheeks.

"Thank you Mr. B. I want to start off by saying that I'm honored and that I will not let the family down." Everyone got up and one by one they hugged and kissed Luca.

Mr. B. had everyone sit down again, "now with my last and final order of business as boss I also want to extend my thanks to the Canadian boys, Joey and Paul. As you know the Canadian Family has brought us all some wealth and we appreciate it. Now I know the boys have some business to discuss with the rest of you so I will give them the floor."

Joey and Paul both got up and addressed the families. Joey looked at Paul and gave him the go ahead to speak. "Men as we all know the drug business has been very successful for us. The last four shipments have brought us all some wealth and we will continue to do so. Our biggest shipment is coming in, in two days from South America and we believe this will be fruitful to all of you. We will of course get in touch with all of you with more details."

Luca just looked at Vinny with disapproval. He had no say in what was going down in the next few days, but he had every intention of putting a stop to this. He wasn't going to ruffle any feathers tonight, however, he was going to hold a meeting and tell the families that this would stop. He had a bad taste in his mouth and didn't like them at all, but for now he had to grin and bear it. Everyone got up and shook their hands and they all extended their appreciation to the Canadians. Luca found himself to feel a little jealous.

Mr. B looked at everyone, "ok men there's music and food out there so go out and enjoy yourself. Luca welcome home." Luca smiled and thanked them all. He walked out and went to look for Bianca out in the garden.

"Babe, why are you sitting out here all alone?"

"Hey you, you kept me waiting long enough, is everything ok?"

"Yeah I had to set those boys straight, did they bother you? What were they saying?"

"Oh they were saying what they were going to do to me when you weren't looking." Nikki gets closer to Luca and put her arms around his neck, "They said they were going to make me scream and have me beg for more."

Luca had fire in his eyes and was ready to run back and kill those two idiots, "I swear I'm going to fuck them up!"

Nikki started to laugh, "come on Luca, do you actually think they would dare say that to me? They were just introducing themselves."

Luca grabbed her by the waist, "if anyone ever gets out of line with you, you have to promise me that you will tell me."

She smiled and kissed him, "I wouldn't hesitate at all. Who were those two idiots anyway, do you know them well?" Luca got her by her hand and they started to walk through the garden.

"Honestly, I don't know them too well. I spoke to them earlier this week before we went to Boston and I have to admit, I'm not a fan. I don't like them and I think they are up to no good."

"Why do you say that?"

"They are from this new Canadian Family that I don't trust. We really don't know a lot about them."

"Really, like what?"

"Babe, what's with all the questions? Do you work for the feds?" Nikki just froze and didn't know what to say. She threw her hands around his neck and thought fast, "yeah babe, and part of my job is to fuck you!"

He laughed, "And you know how to do that very well." He grabbed her face and kissed her. They started to walk and Nikki was relieved. She had to watch herself and what she was saying. Luca looked at her and smiled.

"Honestly, I don't trust easy but there's something about you that makes me feel secure. You seem very sincere and I trust you with my life." Bianca tried not to look away but she felt horrible knowing that she was trying to put them all away and he trusted her with his life.

"I feel the same way, I'll be honest when I first met you at the book store I took you for your typical wanna be gangster, but you are such a good man. You actually are very sincere and honest. You are not like the rest of them."

"Those two goons are no good. I really don't like them but I have to do what the families want."

"Why?"

"It's not that easy. You see there's a huge shipment coming in and I'm not happy about it. They are all into these drugs but I'm so against it. I want nothing to do with it. This was already set up before they gave me this new position. Apparently, this is the fifth shipment that these boys have set up, it's my first shipment, and mark my words, it will be the last."

"Wait what new position are you talking about?" and how long have these guys been around?"

"You are looking at the new Boss of The Buoncuore Family. They have been here a while, they are the "Hook Up" for the families. I'm going to put an end to that after this shipment."

"What! Are you kidding? Mr. Buoncuore made you Boss?" Nikki knew this but she had to act surprised.

"Yes, I'm a big shot now."

Luca gave Nikki a huge proud smile. "Anyway, enough about work, so what do you think of the party?"

Nikki smiled, "I think everyone loves you."

Luca fixed his collar and shows Nikki his signature self kiss, he kisses his hand and with that hand he puts it up to his cheek. He kisses his hand again and puts it up to the other cheek. "Mwha, Mwha, who wouldn't love me?"

Nikki went hysterical with laughter, "OH MY GOD! You got to be kidding me, are you kissing yourself?"

He smiled at her, "Yeah Babe, I love myself."

"I can see that!"

"Unless you want to kiss me?

She leaned over and kisses him, "you are irresistible." He grabbed her really close, "as much as I want to take you away and do nasty things to you, we have to go back to the party."

Nikki pouted and gave him a sad puppy face, "Do we really have to?"

"Oh sweet thing you are so hot when you do that but yes we do. We'll stay a little bit and then we can go."

"Ok just a little bit longer."

They went back in to the party and they mingled a little more. The music was playing and Luca got Nikki and led her to the dance floor. He brought her to the center and with one hand spun her around then pulled her close. Everyone watching started to clap.

Nikki a little taken back with the applause looked around, "Luca why are they clapping, it's not like it's our wedding?"

Luca laughed, "Babe we are the most amazing couple here, people are looking at us with admiration."

Nikki added, "Yeah, and now fear from you."

He kissed her and they clap again. "Wow, this is too funny, they are like show monkeys, can you make them do flips and hang from the chandeliers?"

Luca laughed so loud, "Oh my God you should've been a comedian." The dance floor started to become packed and one by one the couples got closer to them. They were congratulating the happy couple. Nikki was confused,

"It seems like this party went from a welcome home to an engagement party."

"This is their way of welcoming you to the family." They finished their dance and they walked over to Vinny and his date. They were drinking and enjoying the night when Mr. B calls Luca into the room. Luca gave Vinny orders to stay by Bianca and not to let her out of his sight.

"Mr. B. what can I do for you?"

"Luca, I couldn't help but admire you and Bianca, you two seems very much in love."

"Well Mr. B. I won't lie I have a really soft spot for her I do believe I have fallen in love with her."

"Luca, but how long do you know her? I don't mean to pry but you did just get out."

"That's the thing I just met her, but Mr. B I believe that when you meet the person that you are meant to be with for the rest of your life, you just know. It hits you like a bolt of lightning."

"Ok Luca, just be careful. She seems like a really nice girl and I really do hope she's the one. I did promise your father that I would guide you and if you need anything at all, my door is always opened."

"Thank you Mr. B. Listen, we both know that I'm not a fan of drugs and you know this. I plan to make this the last shipment and I want to address the families in a meeting."

"Luca, I told you how the families might feel about this but you're the boss now, all I can do is sit and listen. Now get back out there to that woman of yours before someone steals her."

"I'm actually going to take off. It's been a long night."

"Ok Luca, come by tomorrow we can go over the meeting you plan on having."

"Ok Boss sounds good."

"Luca my boy, you're the boss now not me."

"Yeah I am." They walked out together laughing and the crowd stopped and looked at them.

Mr. B. looked at the crowd, "what happened do I have something coming out of my nose?" They all start to laugh. "Luca the best thing about being the boss is every joke is funny, even if it stinks." They laughed and Luca said his goodbye.

Vinny and his date walked out with Luca and Nikki. Nikki told Maria, Vinny's date, how nice it was to meet her and that they should double one night. Vinny laughed, "yeah, well I think we will all see a lot of each other now." Luca looked at Vinny with a look of approval for his new girl. They said their goodbyes and left.

On the car ride home Nikki was quiet, she was still trying to figure out what those two goons were doing there, but at the same time she was very excited. A shipment was coming in and this was her chance to bust them all. She just looked over at Luca and he smiled. She was trying to figure out how she could avoid busting him. She realized he was heavy in thought.

"What's wrong?"

"Nothing, I was just thinking."

"I thought I smelled wood burning."

Luca laughed, "No really what's wrong Luca, why are you so deep in thought?"

"I was just thinking about this new found responsibility and how many changes I want to make."

"Listen, I think you will be great. You have a lot of good ideas and you want to lead them in the right direction. I believe you have a way with words and you can convince them."

"I hope you're right, I just feel that those two guys from Canada have a lot of pull and it might be hard to convince the families, especially with all the money these guys have brought in for everyone."

"Luca what I don't understand is that you said there have been prior shipments, not to jinx you and the family but how did all these shipment get through without anyone getting caught?"

"Oh Bianca you have to understand, everyone is on the take. They got a few people on the inside of the government that are very corrupt. These drug dealers have people that tip them off on the inside of the law. You will be surprised how many people turn their heads, as long as they are getting a piece of the action."

"So you are saying that some government agents are involved and are on the take?"

"Babe it's sad but yes, there's a lot of money in drugs and some agents see the opportunity and try to get a piece of the action. It's a corrupt world and I hope that I can put an end to it." Nikki was a little shocked. Did the chief know that this is going down? She kept wondering who would do that. She had every intentions of seeing the chief first thing in the morning. She had a lot of questions and was also excited to let him know of the shipment that was coming in. Luca pulled up to Nikki's place. She looked over at him,

"I had a great time tonight."

"Yeah I'm sure you did, waiting around for me until I finished my business."

"No really Luca I did."

"So does that mean you are calling it a night?"

"Yes, I'm sorry I'm really tired and have a long day ahead of me."

"Yes I do too." Luca gave Nikki a big long kiss and promised to call her tomorrow. She walked out and went up to her place.

CHAPTER 17

"I HAVE TO STOP IT! I can't believe it got this far. Why didn't I tell him?" Nikki is driving and its pouring rain, she's trying to get to the old warehouse by the train station. She's passing every light, she doesn't care. She's in tears and all she keeps repeating is, "I have to stop it! Why didn't I tell him?" She comes to a stop, the divider comes down, the train is going to past. She gets out and she screams, "LUCA!" All of a sudden, out of nowhere appear Joey and Paul, Mikes' goons. Paul looks at Joey, "look who it is, did you actually think you were going to win?" Nikki is in tears, "You did this! This is your entire fault!" Paulie gets close to Nikki and whispers in her ear, "You are not all that you Bitch!"

Nikki woke up in a cold sweat, *what the fuck were those two assholes doing in my dream? Something is going down and I have to put a stop to it!* Nikki couldn't stand that she was having these dreams every night. She had to put the pieces together. She got out of bed, showered and headed out, stopping at Starbucks and picked up her Mocha. She was ready to face the chief.

Nikki wasn't sure what was going on. A lot of what Luca was saying last night made some sense. *There were prior shipments, if Mike is in charge and the goons are involved then why didn't they intercept the shipments? What are they waiting for?* The goons were at the headquarters too much and they were the major drug lords last night at the party. People feared them and were paying way too much attention to them. *There is more than what they are telling me and I'm going to find out.*

Is this a conspiracy? All these thoughts were going through her head as she's driving heading to the office. She knew the chief would be pissed but she had to tell him about the shipment. She had to see how involved the department was, she was going to test him. She will tell him about the shipment if he ordered the raid then she knew that he wasn't involved but if it went the other way, she would be very unhappy. She pulled into her spot, took a deep breath and went in. All eyes were on Nikki.

Larry stopped her half way, "Nikki what are you doing here?"

Nikki looked at him, "did you find anything out for me; do they know why those idiots were there?"

Larry's eyes went straight to the floor, "No, nothing."

Nikki rolled her eyes, "Larry, please tell me you are not in on this too?"

"In what?"

"Is the chief around?"

"Yeah, he's in the office, Nikki what aren't you telling me?"

"Just wait for me out here and then I'll tell you." Nikki went to the chief's office and knocked on the door.

"I know that's not you Nikki because you are NOT supposed to be here."

"Chief, can I come in?"

"Do I have a choice?"

"No not really because I'm coming in either way." Nikki walked in and the chief just smiled and shook his head.

"You just can't stay away."

"Well yesterday was the big party and I thought maybe you wanted to know what went down. Oh but wait, you probably know what went down because those two fucking idiots were there!"

"Nikki you need to breathe and relax."

"RELAX, REALLY? What happened to this being my baby? Why were they there?"

"Nikki first of all, I was not going to let you go there unprotected, you needed someone there."

"Oh please chief don't give me that, you know I can handle myself. And what the fuck were those two idiots going to do, hide behind me! Well you will be happy to know that there has been a breakthrough but you already know that too. There's a huge shipment coming in and all the families will be involved, I think this is the perfect time to intercept and take them all down!" Nikki was gleaming, she was so excited. She has been waiting for this moment all her life.

The chief sighed and look down, "No Nikki it's not a good time."

Nikki's face just dropped, she knew that what she feared was true; that the chief had his hands in this and this killed her. "What do you mean it's not a good time? It's the perfect time, it involves everyone! They all go down at once, this is HUGE!" The chief looked up and saw Mike looking into the office and shaking his head.

She looked back to see what he was looking at and saw Mike look away.

"What is going on here?"

"Nikki this is not the time, and we are waiting for something bigger."

"No you're not because there have been four prior shipments, why didn't we intercept those?"

"Those shipments weren't worth it."

"You know what I think; I think this is a conspiracy. I think that we are supplying the mob with drugs! Drugs that we take in as evidence and then you recycle it and make money off of it. I think you and Mike are corrupt and you are using those two fucking idiots to distribute the drugs."

"Nikki you have no idea what you are talking about."

"Oh but I do. How about I get the CIA involved or better yet why don't we get internal affairs involved?"

"Are you threatening me?"

"NO I am making a promise that I will figure it all out and bring you all down!" Nikki slammed the door and walked out. She was pissed and Larry waited a few minutes before following her out. George had just walked in and had no idea what was going on but followed Nikki and Larry.

The chief called in Mike to the office. Mike closed the door, "She figured it out?"

The chief put his hands on his waist and just stared down at his desk, "I didn't want this to happen, but we have to figure out a way to shut her up."

Mike flipped out, "I knew we shouldn't have put her on this case! We did fine for years and now she has to come and ruin it all. You know we have to fix this?"

The chief started rubbing his head, "Fine! Call in Joey and Paulie." Mike violently pulled the door open and walked out.

* * * * *

LUCA STARTED HIS MORNING with a cup of espresso and Vinny banging on the door. "Vin don't you ever sleep?"

Vinny all anxious, "No I'm always up."

"Relax what's wrong with you? Do you want a cup of espresso?"

"Yeah that's all I need, CAFFEINE!"

"OK you are making me nervous and I actually woke up in a good mood. So what the fuck is your problem?"

"Lu, you saw Maria last night, right?"

"Yeah, she's a pretty girl. She's no Bianca, but she's good for you."

"Well I thought so and I brought her home last night."

"That's my boy! You took my advice and got laid but wait Vin, why are you all crazy? You should be relaxed and still at your apartment with Maria!"

"That's the thing, I couldn't do it."

"What are you talking about? Oh, I see you are still thinking about Patricia, she was hot too."

"No, I never did anything with Patricia either."

"What??"

"Luca, I'm nervous."

"Okay Vinny you are making me nervous, what's wrong? You can't get it up?" I mean what the fuck!"

"No, Lu I was starting to get it on with Maria and I just kept thinking of George."

"WOO, who the fuck is George?"

"George Clooney."

Luca just sat there with a stunned face. He just stared at Vinny and then out of nowhere he burst out laughing. "Oh my God, I knew it! Vin, you're gay!"

"No, I can't be! Am I?"

"Yeah man you are!"

"Luca, this is bad, I'm an underboss, I'm a tough fucking gangster, I can't be gay."

"So you're the guy in the relationship." Luca started laughing again, "Oh fuck I did not see this coming, and well actually I did. Listen Vin you are still my best buddy and my right hand man, it doesn't matter what side of the fence you play on. Just don't look at me that way or I will fuck you up, and I don't mean the way you like it!" Luca went hysterical with laughter.

"Luca it's NOT FUNNY!"

"Yeah it is. Vin, relax I won't say a thing I promise." Vinny just looked at his friend and realized what a true and loyal friend he was. Anyone else would've flipped out but he was there for him, and that made Vinny feel better. Luca looked at Vinny, "Listen I'm heading to the studio to meet some of the actors that they attached to this movie, take a ride with me."

Vinny nodded, "Okay."

Luca put his arm around Vinny, "the bright side is that Bianca has a brother, maybe he's gay and I can hook you up." Luca went hysterical again, "I'm sorry Vin you know I have to abuse you for at least a week."

Vinny pulled away, "you're an ass."

He walked away and Luca called out to him with his arms stretched out, "Oh what's the matter I'm not your type? I'm everyone's type. Oh man this is great, I'm going to have fun with this for a while. Oh, Vin wait up, you're driving!" Luca finally caught up with Vinny, "I'm sorry man I'm just trying to process this whole thing."

"Luca, how do you think I feel?"

"I don't know; you have to explain something to me. You see, when I see a hot broad I get blinded by her beauty, heck I'm still fucking blind with Bianca. My question is how do you not get blinded? How do you see it?"

"Luca, I can't explain it either. It's just really fucked up and I'm trying to figure it out myself. Maybe I was just born like this. I always tried to figure out why I was so drawn to George and Brad. I mean I thought they were just really good looking actors but now it's all making sense. Luca what I don't get it is how you didn't flip out?"

"You're my best friend, who cares what you are? Just be yourself and don't let anyone find out. You don't know what these crazy guys will do or react. Oh and another thing, stop staring at my ass."

"WHAT!"

"Yeah, I caught you once or twice, just stop. I know I'm hot but you will make Bianca jealous." Luca couldn't stop laughing.

"That's enough! You are making fun of me."

"No, I'm just trying to make you feel ok about it, and that it doesn't matter to me."

Vinny just smiled at Luca with appreciation. They pulled up to the studio, parked and got out. Vinny turned to Luca, "I still can't believe you are the boss of The Buoncuore Family and starring in a movie."

Luca raised his eyebrows, "I still can't believe you have fantasies of George Clooney." They both laughed and went inside. Mark the producer, was waiting for Luca. He was excited about the movie and that they had Luca attached as Tony, the main guy.

"Luca, how the heck have you been?"

"Mark my man, I'm good. This is my friend Vinny, Vinny this is Mark."

"Nice to meet you Vinny."

"Same here Mark."

"SO Luca are you ready to become a star?"

Luca started to look around and started to see some big names attached to this. "Is that Kevin Dillon?"

Mark turned around to see who Luca was looking at, "Yeah that's him, he will be your right hand man."

Luca was impressed, "Wow, I loved him on Entourage." Mark called over Kevin and introduced the two. Mark had Luca run some lines with Kevin to make sure that they got along, and was very happy with the result.

Vinny was on the side watching his friend and he couldn't believe how good he was. After a few scenes the producer called it a day. Luca walked over to Mark and thanked him.

Mark told him how great the entertainment business was and how much money was involved and how much you could make.

Luca knew this, and it was what he had to try to convince the families of. He said his goodbyes, Mark told Luca to come back next week and they would try to wrap up his part. Luca told Vinny they had to go meet with Mr. B. so they had to leave.

CHAPTER 18

NIKKI TOLD THE BOYS the whole story and her assumption on what was going on with the chief and Mike.

George couldn't believe it, "I don't get it, aren't we the good guys?"

Larry just stared at his coffee, disillusioned, "if you think about it, we are worse than the mob."

George just shook his head, "what I don't understand is why they put you on the case? They know you're not stupid and if anyone would figure it out it would be you."

Nikki looked at them, "when they gave me Luca, they had no clue that he was going to be the next boss they thought I was going to follow around an actor. They had no clue what was going to happen."

Larry finally looked up from his coffee, "So Nikki what are you going to do?"

She held her head high, "Oh we are still working the case, just that now we can't tell the chief and Mike our every move. I have to get internal affairs involved but at the same time we can't blow the case."

George looked at Nikki, "Nik, what's up with you and Luca, you are falling aren't you?" Nikki got up, "George this isn't an episode of *One Life to Live.* So get your ass up and let's get to work." They all got up and got back to work.

*   *   *   *   *

BACK AT THE HEADQUARTERS in the chief's office Mike is sitting there with the two goons and the chief. The chief was very disappointed by the day's events. They were trying to figure out what to do about Nikki. They'd had no clue that Luca would become the boss and that Nikki would figure it all out.

Paulie looked at Mike, "there's only one thing we can do; we have to get rid of her."

The chief shook his head, "I really don't like doing that, I mean to actually get rid of one of our own?"

Mike looked at him, "She's not one of us chief. She's just getting in the way."

"Yeah but we can't have her blood on our hands Mike."

Joey agreed and had a better idea, "we just have to let the families know that she's a fed. Then they will have no choice but to get rid of her. That way we don't have the blood on our hands and if it ever comes out, we get them for killing a fed."

The Chief liked the idea, "but how will you convince Luca? He is blinded and in love with her."

A nefarious smile crosses Paulie's face, "we get pictures of her at the station with one of you. You call her back in and you tell her you want to discuss the case. She comes we snap pictures."

Joey smiled, "that's not a bad idea Paulie, but how will we explain how we got the pictures from inside the station? We have to take them while she's outside, that way we can say we were tailing her."

Paulie nodded, "you're right, that's not a bad idea. Okay, so chief you need to get her in here and meet her outside; you or Mike it doesn't matter who. Once we get evidence we go to Luca and the families with it and they have to get rid of her. Luca hates rats so he will have no choice." They all smiled with sinister intent and put the plan in motion.

* * * * *

NIKKI HEADS BACK TO the apartment all distraught about everything. As she was walking in, her cell phone rang. Looking at the caller ID, she saw that it was Luca. Smiling, she answered it.

"Hello."

"Oh sweet thing, I missed that voice today."

"Hey Luca, how are you?"

"I'm better now that I heard your voice." Nikki smiled but Luca sensed that she was upset, "what's wrong Bianca, is everything ok?"

"Yeah just a bad day at the office."

"How about I swing by later and make it up to you?"

"I don't know if I will be good company. Honestly, I haven't worked out and wouldn't mind stepping in the ring for a little boxing."

"Babe, Boxing? Listen let me set it up and we can go do a few rounds. I have a meeting in a little bit but I'll swing by in an hour and we can go to my private gym."

"You have a private gym?"

"You keep forgetting who you are talking to.

"Yes I do."

"Get ready and I'll pick you up in an hour."

"Okay, that sounds good."

"Chin up, you will see me in an hour and Luca will make it all better."

Nikki smiled to herself and hung up.

*   *   *   *   *

LUCA AND VINNY ARRIVED at Mr. Buoncuore's Estate. They got out of the car and were welcomed with opened arms. The cleaning staff was there cleaning up the mess from the night before, but that didn't stop Mrs. B. from making her famous Sunday lunch. She smiled and hugged the boys, "boys you are just in time, we were going to sit down to eat."

Luca had completely forgotten and now felt bad that he walked in during lunch. "Oh Mrs. B I'm sorry, I didn't mean to barge in like this; I forgot it was Sunday.

Mrs. B waved her hand, "Oh Luca come on you know I'm used to this already and I always make extra. Have a seat and have some lasagne with us."

Luca moans, "Oh as good as that sounds, we really can't stay long I'm meeting Bianca in an hour."

Mrs. B grabbed Luca by the face, "Oh I really like her I hope you hold on to this one, she seems like a keeper."

Luca smiled, "thank you, I think she might be the one."

Vinny hit him on the arm, "who are you kidding? You knew that the moment you met her. You couldn't stop saying, "Oh she's the mother of my children." Everyone started laughing as Vinny grabbed a piece of garlic bread and stuffed his face. She shows them to the office and Mr. B was sitting there waiting for them. She looked at the boys, reminding them "there's plenty of food, so if you change your mind, don't hesitate."

Luca thanked her and she closed the door. Mr. B gets up and hugged Luca and Vinny;

"How are you boys doing today?"

"Good Mr. B couldn't be better."

"So Luca tell me what's on your mind."

"Well you know that I plan to sit down with the five families and discuss this drug business. As you know I'm not a huge fan. I think we can make money in a more legit way."

"You mentioned this before but you never told me what you have in mind. Luca you know that the drug business has brought in a lot of money, and the families are very well off. As a matter of fact I think now is the time for you to get a piece of it. You're a boss now and you're still in an apartment. It's time for you to step up and make some money for yourself."

"Mr. B I'm proud of where I am, and I'm glad that I never had to get into the drug business to make my money. I'm happy where I am, but now that I'm boss, I can't promote this. I think we can make money through the entertainment business."

"Luca what are you talking about?"

"Well when I was in the joint I got into books and I became close with one of the guys. His uncle is a producer and wants to star me in one of his movies."

"Are you serious? Do you know the kind of exposure we will get? The families will not like this!"

"Hear me out, we have the casinos and we have the clubs and that alone brings in enough money. We get into the movies and can you imagine the money we can bring in with that? Of course whatever percentage we get, we distribute to the five families. Between writing, producing and acting and even the music industry, we will make more money than the drugs. The feds will have a hard time pinning shit on us because everything we'll be doing will be legal."

Mr. B. was really sceptical but saw what Luca was talking about. "Luca you will really have to convince the families, and I don't know if they will buy it, you are going to create enemies."

Luca looked at Vinny and back at Mr. B., "I really believe we can make this work."

Mr. B. looked at the boys, still uncertain, "listen set up your meeting. The families will be in Vegas tomorrow for the opening of the new hotel, so why don't you hold it there tomorrow and see how they react. The shipment is due to come in on Wednesday; you know that's still going to happen."

Luca looked down, "yeah I know. I can't stop that, but going forward I want to. I don't want to keep you from your lunch so go enjoy, and I will have Vinny set the meeting up." Mr. B. nodded and once again extended the invitation to stay and eat but Luca kindly declined and thanked him.

In the car Luca gave Vinny his first orders, "Vin, call the families and tell them that tomorrow in Vegas I'm going to hold my first meeting."

"Luca are you sure about this? Mr. B is right. You are going to create enemies. Maybe it's time to get into the drug business and get some real houses and some nice stuff."

Luca smacked Vinny across the head, "you will have all that just that the way I plan to do it, and you will be able to enjoy it instead of being locked up behind bars. Now do what I told you and set up the meeting. I'm going to get Bianca, we are going to work out."

Vinny chuckled, "is that what you guys call it?"

Luca gave him a look, "no jerk off we are really going to work out. She boxes, did you know that?"

Vinny shook his head, "No."

Luca smiled "yeah my girl is a tough bitch. I'm taking her to Sonny's gym for a little one on one."

Vinny grinned, "you guys are nuts but I have to admit, you make a good couple."

"Yeah I know. I'm going to take her to Vegas with us. You want me to ask her if she wants to bring her brother?"

Vinny gave Luca a sharp, mean scowl, "You see I shouldn't have told you shit!"

Luca laughed, "I'm kidding buddy, I'm only kidding." Luca dropped Vinny off and told him to make the phones calls and check on the airline tickets. Vinny nodded and went inside, while Luca took off and headed to Nikki's place.

* * * * *

NIKKI DRESSED IN HER gym clothes and waited for Luca. She really needed a good workout to release some stress. Just as she was finishing off dressing, there was a knock on the door. She opened it and a messenger stood there.

"Nikki Jacobs?"

"Yes that's me."

"You need to sign right here." Nikki signed, and then grabbed the envelope, looked at it and just laughed.

The messenger stood there just admiring Nikki and smiling at her. He said, "You've been served."

Then he heard a voice from behind him. "Yo buddy what are you waiting for? You delivered what you had to, so stop staring and go."

The messenger looked over at Luca, "sorry sir.'

Luca gave him a warning look, "yeah you should be, now go!"

Nikki rolled her eyes, like a mother would with an incorrigible child, *oh lord, there he goes again.* She stood there with the big brown envelope in her hand and just smiled wearily at Luca, then shook her head and went inside. He followed her in,

"What? I can't claim what's mine?"

"I told you I'm not a possession, I'm a person."

"Yeah, and you're mine. Anyway, what's that?"

She looked and smiled, "divorce settlement." Luca grabbed Nikki by her waist, "so now you're officially mine!"

She pulled away, "you don't own me."

Luca gave her the once over in her workout outfit, biting his lower lip, "mmmmmm, you look so hot! Come on Babe let's go release some stress because you sound a little testy."

Nikki dropped the envelope, grabbed her gym bag and they were off.

They got to the gym and Nikki looked around, Luca noticed the puzzled look on her face.

"What's wrong, are you ok?"

"There's no one here?"

"Just you and me Babe, I said one on one."

"Yes but I thought there would be other people here"

"Is this a problem, did you want to add a third person because you know I can have that arranged."

Nikki got really close to Luca, "Sure if it's another man."

Luca pulled away, "Oh no Babe, no other man is touching my woman!"

"OH but it's ok to have another woman in the picture?"

"I never said I was going to touch the other woman, we can make her watch."

Nikki reached into her bag and got her gloves out, "Come on, we are here to work out not talk about the only thing that is on your mind."

Luca picked up her chin and looked at Nikki straight in the eyes, "Babe, you are the only thing on my mind."

They started to kiss, Nikki started to get a little hot for Luca so she pulled away, "we are here to box, so get your gloves on and let's see what you got!"

Luca let out a loud chuckle, "Oh man that's the funniest thing I've ever heard, you think you can take me?"

Nikki put up her dukes with her pink gloves on, "Oh I know I can."

Luca stared at the gloves, "PINK? Really? Ooooh you're going down." They both get in the ring and start to prance around each other. Nikki gave Luca her signature smile and he put his guard down and just bit his bottom lip. Nikki saw her opportunity and threw a right hook leaving Luca standing in shock.

"Oh that was sneaky, is that how you are going to play?"

Nikki smiled, "Okay, that was bad, I'm sorry. Let's start over." They began again, Nikki and threw a left hook, but this time Luca ducked, grabbed her by the waist and pinned her to the mat.

"Now I like this."

"You said we were going to box not wrestle."

"I like this position better."

Nikki flipped Luca and straddled over him pinning his arms down.

Luca had a huge smile on his face, "I stand corrected and this is my favorite position." He freed his arms, pulled himself up and started to kiss her. Nikki tried to be all tough and fight him off but she couldn't resist him, and just gave in. Luca took her gloves off and continued to kiss her. Nikki still on top of Luca starts to tease him and whispers in his ear, "I want you right here, right now!"

Luca grabbed her by her hips and just brought her closer. "I'm so glad I made this a private session."

Nikki still kissing Luca, whispered again, "I wouldn't mind if we had an audience." Luca lost it and ripped her clothes off.

She started to laugh, "The littlest thing turn you on."

Luca put his finger on her lips,

"Shhh let's just enjoy this and leave the audience for another day."

"Wow you really just want me all to yourself, don't you?"

"You are my everything. I enjoy every minute with you." She started to kiss him and they made love.

Nikki looked at Luca, "That was some work out?"

"That was off the hook!"

"You know I really was looking forward to a good boxing match with you."

"You wanna go another round?"

"Now that is very tempting." Nikki got on top of Luca again.

"Babe I don't know where you get it but you got some Stamina."

"What's the matter you can't handle me?"

"Oh no, it's you I worry about, can you handle me?"

"Well let me show you." Luca laughed and kissed her, "Sweet thing let's save it for Vegas." Nikki very confused looks at Luca, "VEGAS?"

"Didn't I tell you we were going to Vegas tomorrow?"

"Ah NO you didn't! Luca what are you talking about?"

"Me, you and Vinny are taking a little trip to Vegas, I have some business there I have to take care of and I figured we make it a little get away for us."

"Luca, you can't do that! You can't just assume that I can pick up and go whenever you want."

"You know who you are dating, right?"

"Enough with that! I'm serious, I do have a life and a job and you can't just assume that I can drop everything for you!"

"Wait a minute, are we fighting?"

"Yes we are!" Nikki got up and started to get dressed. She knew she had to go to Las Vegas, it was her job, but she was so furious that he didn't even ask her and that he assumed she would go!

"I got the ticket and I thought that you would love it."

"I'm sorry, I don't mean to snap but I hate it when you think I'm some kind of possession or someone who will just drop everything. I know exactly who you are and that doesn't give you the right to tell me what to do, or other people for that matter."

"What are you talking about?"

"I'm like the fire hydrate that you pee on, if someone comes close they smell your scent and stay away!"

"Babe I would NEVER pee on you but that is funny." Nikki got up all furious and mad but, Luca couldn't help but laugh. He loved this side of Nikki. "Wow, I never saw you this mad, you are actually more sexy when you get mad." Luca grabbed her and tried to calm her down. "Listen to me, I'm really sorry that I didn't ask, and it was wrong of me to assume that you would just drop everything and go with me. I'm asking you now, I know I got the ticket and the amazing suite, BUT I can cancel all that and just go to my meeting. I just don't want to be this far from you."

"Why, because you can't watch what I'm doing?"

"Oh no, I have plenty of people who can do that for me when I'm away."

"LUCA!"

"You're SOOOO STUPID! Bianca I love you so much that when you're not around I feel like I can't breathe. Ok I'm being selfish, and again I'm sorry but I wish you would reconsider and come with us."

"I really didn't take you for the gambling kind."

"I hate gambling and hate being around it. It's sad and pathetic but we are having a meeting and I need to be there, so please come with me?"

"Well if you put it that way, and if you promise that next time you will ask and not just assume?"

"Yes I promise."

"Ok then I will come." Nikki was actually very excited she knew that all the families would be there for Luca's first meeting, and she had to call Larry and tell him what was going down. "So when are we leaving?"

"Luca didn't know himself because Vinny was making all the plans but he knew it was tomorrow, "most likely tomorrow afternoon."

Nikki smiled, "You are giving me no time at all to pack."

"You don't need much. I don't plan on leaving our suite at all."

"Ok then take me home, I need to shower and put some stuff together for tomorrow."

"How about I stay the night, we can shower together and then have dessert."

"What are you in the mood for?"

"YOU!"

"Sounds like a great idea but you need to pack too." Nikki was thinking she needed time to talk to Larry and have him and George come down with her. This meeting needed to be taped. "How about you drop me off? I need to make a few calls to work and take the time I need, and you go home and pack."

"As long as you promise me that you will wait to take your shower."

"I promise."

CHAPTER 19

LUCA DROPPED NIKKI OFF and went to his place to get his bag together. Nikki ran upstairs knowing she didn't have too much time. Quickly, she called Larry to fill him on the plan.

"Larry what are you doing?"

"I'm here waiting for you to call, what's going on?"

"Listen get your bag together we are going to Vegas tomorrow."

"WHAT?"

"Luca is setting up a meeting with the five families and I need you and George to be there so we can get this all on tape."

"Nikki you realize this is tomorrow?"

"Yes, and we can get clearance to go, Larry just get it done. I will call you tomorrow morning with all the information."

"Ok boss, I'll talk to you tomorrow."

Nikki got off the phone and started to get her bag ready for tomorrow. She was still thinking about the chief and how betrayed she felt, but she was determined to bring everyone down. Just as she was finishing up there was a knock on the door, and she couldn't help but smile because she knew it was Luca. She opened the door and Luca was standing there with a huge grin on his face, "Honey I'm home."

Nikki smiled and let him in.

"Did you pack? I hope you didn't take a shower yet."

Nikki looked at herself noting that she was still in her work out clothes, "does it look like I did?"

He grabbed her and kissed her, "Are you being a wise ass with me?"

"Yeah, you are starting to rub off on me."

"Ouch that hurts! You think I'm a wise ass?"

"Who you? Luca Marchisio, No not you Luca! Do you know who you are?" Nikki rolled her eyes and walked into the kitchen. "Would you like a glass of wine?"

He raised his eyebrow, "actually I would, thank you. Babe are you making fun of me?" Nikki's back was turned towards him and a sneaky smile was on her face, "no, me never. So tell me, what's this meeting about?"

Luca just looked at Nikki a little shocked that she would even ask, "just business, you know your usual stuff." She took a sip of wine and just stared at Luca in the eyes.

"I see."

"What does that mean?"

"Nothing, stuff you can't talk about. That's fine I don't need to know anything."

"Listen how about that shower?"

"Why, do I smell?"

"No, I just want to hold you while the water is hitting us."

"Is that all you want to do, just hold me?"

"Yeah ok because that's all I'll be able to do. Do you realize that I can't keep my hands off of you?"

"No, I haven't noticed."

"So how about it, should we go shower?" Just as he finished the sentence Nikki was already getting up and walking towards the bathroom. She peeked out of the door and with her finger, beckoned him in.

"You don't have to tell me twice." Luca bolted off the couch and headed towards the bathroom. Inside the bathroom they started to undress each other. The shower was already running and Luca couldn't help but stare at Nikki's body. "Babe your body is slamming!" She just smiled and entered with him following her in. The water started to hit her wetting her and Luca couldn't help but grab her by her hair and start kissing her. His hands were all over her. She in turn couldn't keep her hands off him. Luca grabbed the body wash and rubbed it all over her body enjoying every touch and biting his bottom lip the whole time. "You are the most beautiful woman in the world." Nikki grabbed the wash and starts to rub it all over him, enjoying every touch. She then grabbed him and he just laughed, "Yeah that's what I'm talking about." He turned her around and started to rub the wash all over her back. He was pressed against her, the water hitting them both and she was getting really turned on, as she felt how excited he was getting.

Luca was still pressed against her back and washing her front touching every part of her body. He started to massage and she couldn't help but moan, enjoying every minute. He bent her over and proceeded to pleasure her even more. Now inside her and making her love it, Luca grabbed her by her waist and kept going in deeper and deeper. Nikki was losing control and could help herself. Luca then turned her around and wrapped her long legs around him. They were both ready to reach their climax. He pulled her hair back and she screamed for more. He kissed her neck as they both climaxed together. They stood under the water just holding each other for a little bit. Then Luca pulled her face up, "I love you so much."

Nikki smiles but with sad eyes, "Luca I love you too, always forever and Eternity." She knew that this will end once he found out who she really was, and she feared that day. However, she wanted him to know that she would always love him.

"Babe, that's pretty deep, you okay?"

Nikki looked up at him, "Yes, I just want to savour all our moments."

Luca stared at her, "I'm not going anywhere I will always be here."

They washed up and got dressed for bed. Vinny touched base with Luca and told him that they are leaving early afternoon and that the meeting would start at seven. Giving them enough time to check in, get changed and head to the meeting. Nikki got all the information and texted Larry. Larry and George were going to take an earlier flight out so they can scope out the place. They were all staying at the Bellagio.

Nikki was having her usual nightmare about driving in the rain and hearing a gunshot. She woke up in a cold sweat screaming "LUCA!"

He jumped out of bed, "Ok babe listen we need to work on this, you can't be giving me heart attacks in the middle of the night."

She looked at him and just hugs him. "Oh Bianca are you ok? What's wrong?"

Nikki with tears in her eyes, "I had a bad dream and I'm just glad you're here."

He kissed her forehead and just held her tight, "Babe its ok, I told you I'm not going anywhere." Suddenly Nikki jumps out of bed and ran to the bathroom. Luca got so nervous and followed her. He heard her throwing up, "Bianca you are making me nervous, are you okay?"

Nikki lifted her head and assured him that she was fine and would be out in a minute. He waited for her outside the door, and when she came out he just hugged her. "What's wrong, why did you get sick?"

She just smiled, "I guess the thought of you not being here makes me sick."

He didn't laugh, "Bianca, don't ever say that again, I will never leave. Now let's get to bed and please, no more nightmares."

She nodded and walked back to bed.

The next morning Nikki woke up to the smell of eggs and bacon. She found herself starving but she took one sniff and she was running in the bathroom again. When she came out Luca looked at her, "what's up with all the puking? Are you allergic to me or something?" She stood there holding her stomach, "I must be catching something; this weather is crazy." He picked up the pan, "do I dare to ask if you want some?"

She smiled, "yes I'm starving."

He got a plate and served her, "good because protein is good for you and you need some after all the working out we have been doing. Will you be ok today on the plane, with your stomach being all weird and all."

Nikki took one bite of the eggs, "yes I'm a big girl I'll be fine."

Luca sat next to her, "okay so hurry up, let's eat. Vinny is picking us up in an hour."

They finished their breakfast and got ready. Nikki wasn't feeling all that great but she was still very excited to be going to Las Vegas. This was a big night and no stomach bug was going to mess it up. Luca let Vinny in while Nikki finished getting ready.

"Vin, my man, is everything set up?"

"Yes, I got the tickets, the suites are all booked and now the only thing we need is to get to the airport."

"What time is the flight?"

"Eleven couldn't get a later flight, plus it's a six hour flight and the meeting is at seven so we are just making it." Nikki walked out and seeing Vinny, she walked over and gave him a big hug and kiss.

"Hey Vin how are you?"

"Ciao Bella, I'm doing good; how about you?"

"I'm good, very excited about Vegas."

Vinny looked over at Luca, "yeah we all are."

Luca gave Vinny a look, "ok first of all, you can't touch my woman like that again and second of all we have to go, so let's go."

Nikki frowned at Luca, "what did I tell you about that?"

Luca laughed, "What? I guess my scent isn't strong enough and I had to remind Vinny that you're my fire hydrant."

Vinny look perplexed at the both of them, "what the fuck are you weirdo's talking about now? Actually, I don't want to know about your crazy sex talk. Let's go we are going to miss the plane." Vinny grabbed the bags and just stared at Luca, "fire hydrant?"

Luca laughed, "forget it Vin you don't want to know."

They got to the plane and settled in; of course Vinny booked all first class, nothing but the best for the new boss. Luca was very impressed that his first orders to Vinny were executed very well. They slept through the whole flight being that they didn't get much sleep the night before. Just as they were waking up the plane was getting ready to land. Luca looked at Nikki who was just waking up, "good afternoon sweet thing how are you feeling?"

Nikki stretched and smiled at him, "like a million bucks."

He kissed her, "you are my treasure."

They didn't have much time so they went to the room. Luca got changed while Nikki just lay on the bed admiring the suite.

"This is truly a nice place, I can get used to this?"

He was adjusting his tie and looking at her through the mirror, "Nothing but the best for my woman." He kissed her and told her that he would be back and that she should get into something really sexy and maybe orders some room service. She nodded and he left. The minute the door closed behind him, she called Larry.

"Ok he just left, is everything set up?"

"Yes. We didn't want to bug the room because we figured they would find them and remove them, so George and I will be bringing in a cart of food and drinks. The cart will have a bug so you can also hear it."

"Good job guys."

"Nikki you really want to bust Luca?"

"It's not Luca I'm after anymore, he's harmless but I do plan to bring the rest down."

"Ok please call me if anything happens, George and I are here, OK?"

"Yes of course."

* * * * *

VINNY AND LUCA WALKED into the meeting and all the guys are there waiting. Everyone walked over and said hello. Carlo DeVito from Boston was there; the biggest drug family in the organization. Dominick "mimmo" Locasi was there; he owned the biggest pizzeria chain in the east coast. Louie Romano from New Jersey, who also had a chain of restaurants, was working the room. Mikey Gallo from Staten Island, who ran an import and export business for Italian foods, and last but not least Peter Russo from Brooklyn; he was also in the import and export business. The two goons were also there, Joey and Paul. Luca wasn't too happy to see them but was very happy to see everyone else. After their small talk on how the families were doing and how the kids were getting so big they all sat down to discuss business. Luca stood and started his meeting.

"First of all I would like to thank all of you for coming on short notice. I know tonight is the big night for the New hotel and I'm sure it will do very well. Good Luck to the Gallo family and hopefully it's very profitable for all of us." Just as he was talking two waiters walked in to drop off a cart of drinks and food for the guys.

Peter stared angrily at them, "Oh what the fuck are these waiters doing?"

One of the goons recognized Larry, "its ok guys I had them bring up some champagne and food." They all looked at each other.

Luca continued, "Thank you guys that will be all." George and Larry walked out; "As I was saying, thank you again for meeting me on short notice. I wanted to talk to you about the narcotics in our organization. As you all know we are bringing in a lot of cash and I'm sure you are all doing well."

Carlo interrupted, "I'm sorry Luca I know you haven't been around and if you feel you are not getting a fair cut we can always accommodate you. As you know we are getting a huge shipment tomorrow and there will be enough for everyone to share."

Everyone looked at each with pleasure knowing that more money will be coming in.

Luca resumed, "Actually that's not why I held this meeting, it's part of it but not the main reason. You all know that I'm not a huge fan of narcotics. I was never for it and I know it's a business, people choose to do it but we all know that eventually it will end up in high schools and in the hands of young kids. This is the problem that bothers me; I can't sleep at night knowing that some kid can die because of me. Carlo thank you, but my family will not be involved. Now that I am boss, I've decided that I will be doing things a lot different. Carlo you can actually have my cut."

The guys all looked at each other in shock; Peter Russo who was an older man questioned Luca,

"Luca but what are you talking about? Does Buoncuore Family know you decided this?"

"It doesn't matter they will do as I say, I'm the boss now. I don't like the drug business, I think it's dirty, and it's giving it to young kids who go out and end up killing themselves. I want to be able to sleep at night."

Carlo looked around the room, "And what do you suggest we do?"

"I'm not suggesting you do anything, I decided to take my family in a different route. A route that will generate a lot more money, a route that will make us all enjoy it outside of prison. What good is money if you have to be behind bars? And really let's think about it if you get caught what do you think the feds will do? Mimmo tell me how many pizzerias do you own?"

"I have a few you know that, but what does that have to do with anything?"

"Well the feds will take all your pizzerias away, all your money. What about you Louie, how many restaurants do you have? They will rip them all away from you. Now tell me what are your wives and children going to do when you are in the joint and they don't have a pot to piss in? Who's going to help them?"

Mikey was starting to see where he was going with this but he also knew this was the risk they took. "But Luca what do you plan to do? How do plan to make all this money?"

"I'm looking into the entertainment business."

Carlo smirked, "we already have strip joints." Everyone in the room started to laugh.

Luca focused his attention on Peter DeLuca, "I'm talking about the film industry, the music business. It's a growing industry and in the long run we will be making more money than we would selling drugs."

Peter got his attention, "how do you figure that?"

"My family has a lot of connections in the movie business; we can tap into and get a piece of the action. We would be doing something legit and it would drive the feds crazy trying to pin shit on us."

Peter looked over to Louie, "you know Tony Rizzo is into the film industry."

Louie nodded, "that's right he's a producer or something like that."

Mikey nodded, "my nephew Nicky is actually trying to get into the acting thing maybe we can hook him up."

Luca smiled, "you see what I'm talking about, Staten Island, Brooklyn, Queens is full of young Italians who are trying to make it in this industry, who better but us Italians to make it big and it's legit, and we help out our families along the way. Don't you want to see the Italian actors back on the big screen, a future Deniro or Al Pacino? What do you think they were doing in the fifties, Sinatra, Tony Bennett, Joe DiMaggio, the drugs came in and everything went to shit? Yes we were making money but half of us got locked up and couldn't enjoy it. We start to introduce our guys to producers or music agents and bang they make it big. Of course we get a percentage of it and everyone is happy."

The goons were not happy with the way things are going, they saw that Luca is swaying the guys away from the drugs and ruining all their hard work.

Joey the goon chimed in, "yeah but in the long run. What about now, who's going to pay your bills now? How long are you talking about?"

Luca looked at him; "I think right now we are all pretty well off, we have the casinos, our restaurants all our business, that in the meantime pays your bill. We got this new hotel in Vegas. I have to say I think we are doing pretty well for ourselves." Carlo shakes his head, "yeah well most of my business is drugs, and I make a lot of money."

"Yes but tell me what good is all that money if you get pinched? It's worthless because they will take it and leave your wife and kids with nothing."

Peter looked at Carlo, "I have to say I like this, because I have grandkids and I would love to enjoy them from the outside world not behind bars. And frankly selling drugs doesn't make me sleep well either; you know what they say, once you play in mud long enough you will eventually get stained."

Luca adjusted his suit and smiled, "And you know me, I don't like to get dirty."

Peter laughs, "Luca I have to say this isn't a bad idea, and this is something that I will consider." Luca nodded and smiled. Louie too agreed and liked the idea. Carlo was furious, the drug business was his money maker and the idea of him giving it up gave him a bad taste in his mouth. "I don't Luca. I don't think the entertainment world is for me."

"Listen I'm not telling you all what to do, I'm simply telling you that my family will not be participating in the narcotics anymore. You wanted to know what my plans were and I'm telling you. If you want to pursue this with me I will be more than happy to share." Mimmo, Mikey and Carlo were not jumping on any band wagon just yet. They liked the fast money they were making and were too afraid to lose the comfort zone they were in. The goons were fuming. They didn't like it at all. Luca looked at everyone, "Listen boys change is good and sometimes it's for the best. Why do you always have to give the feds a reason, fuck them! Let's stick it to them, let them work hard and try to pin something on us! We work hard at what we do. Who the fuck are they to just come in and take it all away? If we do it the right way we will not be giving them any reason. Fuck, they will be out of a job not us! We will be walking the red carpet and rubbing elbows with all those famous people. Peter didn't you say you knew George Clooney?"

Peter smiled, "yes we met up in Italy, he was on vacation and we got to talking and now we talk every now and then."

Luca looked at Carlo, "you see we are already in the industry, why not make some money out of it? Listen boys you think about it and let me know." Everyone got up and shook hands, some of them were happy and some weren't so keen on the idea, but overall Luca felt good about the meeting. He got through to Peter Russo and he was an older man with a lot of pull and experience. Luca knew that if he could get to Peter, the others would follow. He came and did what he wanted to do and was very happy about it. Mikey announced to everyone that the hotel was opened and that he welcomed everyone to come out tonight and enjoy it. Everyone nodded and said goodbye.

Luca and Vinny started to head back to their rooms. Vinny stopped Luca, "Lu tell me something, you don't like gambling you don't like narcotics but what the fuck kind of boss are you?"

Luca looked at him, his expression serious, "the kind that's going to make you a lot of money and keep your ass out of jail, even though now that I think about it, you might actually like it in there."

Vinny gave Luca a dirty look, "Oh fuck you, I'm never telling you anything again. I'm going to play some blackjack, you coming? "

"Really Vin? You know how much I hate gambling, why are you going to go piss your money away like that?"

"Because I enjoy it and I feel lucky tonight."

"Yeah so do I, and she's waiting for me in my suite!"

Vinny rolled his eyes, "yeah go enjoy your Bianca."

"You're just jealous I'm getting laid and you're not!"

"Lu really you're going there again?"

"Ok I'm sorry, go piss your money away, I'll talk to you later."

CHAPTER 20

NIKKI WAS VERY HAPPY with what she heard in the meeting. She knew that Luca was a good person who was trying really hard to change the ways of the family. She couldn't have been more proud of him. She also knew that tomorrow's shipment was very huge and that those goons were up to no good. She left orders for Larry and George to keep an eye on them from a distance. Just as she put her listening apparatus away Luca walked in.

"Babe! I missed you so much." He walked over to her and gave her the biggest hug and kiss as if he hadn't seen her for months.

"I missed you too, how did your meeting go?"

He smiled, "it went exactly as I planned."

Nikki patted him on the back, "good for you, I'm really happy for you."

"I did miss you very much Bianca, what did you do while I was gone?"

"I actually ordered some room service and they should be up shortly, and then I just sat here and watched TV."

"I'm starving what did you order?"

"SUSHI."

"You are so good to me! I'm going to jump in the shower, would you like to join me?"

"I'll wait for you out here just in case the food comes."

"What? You are turning me down?"

"No I would never do that, but I want to warm up the bed for you."

"Okay that's fine, I'll be right out."   Nikki had to make sure everything was put away securely and that he wouldn't find any of it.

Luca didn't take long in the shower.   He came out dripping wet and with just a towel wrapped around his waist.   Nikki was lying in bed when she turned around to see him just standing there.   She admired his six foot three body with wash board abs.   He wasn't huge but he was toned, and just perfect.   She found herself biting her lower lip and letting out a small little moan.   Luca looked at her a little surprised, "Do you want some of this?"

She started to laugh so hard, "Babe you ruined it, I was just picturing George Clooney and then you had to go and open your mouth."

Luca's face just dropped, "what the fuck does this George Clooney have that I don't?"

Nikki got up, went over to him and put her arms around his muscular waist, "Don't be jealous, he's like make believe. I will never meet him."

Luca hugging her back, stared into her eyes, "Babe anything is possible, I can make it happen."

She raised her eyebrows, "Umm a threesome?"

He started to fidget just at the thought of someone else touching her, "if that's what you want, how would you feel if there was another woman?"

Nikki knew that this is killing him and that no man can touch her but him, "If that's what you want, then I don't see why not. Will I get my George if I say yes?"

Luca knowing that she will never do the threesome agreed. She started to play around with Luca and ripped his towel off, leaving him standing there butt naked, "Oh baby you are HOT!"

Luca started to struts his stuff around the room, "Yeah, I know."

Nikki grabbed a pillow and threw it at him. Just as he caught the pillow there was a knock on the door, *"Room Service."* Nikki started to laugh and twirled the towel around not giving it to Luca.

"Babe come on I'm naked."

Nikki opened the door with Luca hiding behind her trying to cover himself.

The waitress blushed, "I'm sorry I thought you said come in."

Nikki smiles, "I did; you can put the cart in there." The waitress felt a little uncomfortable going in there while Luca was butt naked. Nikki was just having fun with it. As the waitress wheeled the cart inside room Nikki turned to Luca, "Oh babe you are making me so hot standing here all naked." She started to kiss and touch him all over.

Luca confused at what she was doing, said, "Babe we have company, how about we wait until she leaves."

Nikki frowned and pouts, "I have an idea, why doesn't she stay and watch?"

The waitress raised her eyebrows, "Ah, I'm really sorry the door was opened and I thought—"

Nikki didn't let her finish, "It's ok but you are welcomed to stay and watch if you want, make it your tip for the service."

Luca just looked at Nikki, questioning, "Babe, were you drinking when I was in the shower? Did you smoke anything funny while I was at my meeting?"

Nikki whispered in his ear, "If I do this I can have George so I'm giving you what you want."

Luca laughed really hard, "So that's what this all about, I knew you were up to no good."

Nikki looked at the waitress, "So? Want to hang out with us for a few drinks and a show?" The waitress feeling the tension looked at both of them and smiled, "no thank you, but thanks for the offer." Then she left.

Nikki closed the door and stared at her naked man.

He stuck out his hand; "How about you give me back the towel."

She grinned and threw it in the bathroom.

He looked at her with a wicked sexy smile, "I see you are in a playful mood tonight. Why don't you tell me what was that all about with the waitress, are you serious about this threesome?"

Nikki looked at Luca, "You know just as much as you hate someone touching me that is how much I hate someone touching you. I don't like to share and I don't want another woman touching my man! So let's get this straight that a threesome is out of the question and will never happen."

Luca all naked grabbed Nikki and kissed her, "I love you so much Bianca and I'm glad we are on the same page because as much as women think that men are into these things, I'm one of the few that enjoys my woman and just my woman." Just as he finished his sentence Nikki ran to the bathroom and threw up. Luca stood by the bathroom door asking her if she was okay. "Babe what's going on, every time I tell you my feelings, you puke?"

Nikki came out laughing, "You're so silly Luca, you know I have some kind of a stomach bug. Actually I did pretty well all day."

He just smiled and hugged her but he was still very worried about her, he didn't like it that she wasn't feeling well. "Let's just go to bed, it's been a long day and you need some rest." She nodded and they went to bed.

Much later Nikki was awakened by a lot of commotion going on outside. She didn't want to wake Luca up, so she looked outside to see what was going on. Her hand went to her mouth in initial horror as she saw Vinny standing on the ledge of the building.

"It's not worth living, why me?"

Nikki quickly went back in woke up Luca, "Luca, Luca wake up!"

Luca jumps up, "Oh no are you having another nightmare about me?"

"NO it's Vinny, please Luca get up!"

Luca jumped out of bed and threw on his sweats.

"What's wrong with Vinny?"

"His outside the ledge saying it's not worth it."

"What the fuck is he thinking? We are on the 50th floor!"

Nikki and Luca walked over to Vinny's room and he was outside the ledge still crying, "Why me? How can this happen?"

"Yo Vin, what's going on? You realize its forty degrees outside?"

"Luca I swear I'm going to jump!"

"Why, can you just tell me what's going on?"

"I just can't, I blew everything; everything is gone!"

"Vin there's a lot of guys who are gay, WHO CARES!"

"What are you talking about? You think I'm going to jump because I think I'm gay?"

"Yeah, why else would you wake my ass up in the wee hours of the night?"

"Luca I was playing poker and I lost a lot of money, I mean a lot of money!"

"Vin, listen why don't you come in and we can talk about it, it's cold out there and I have no shirt on."

"No, there's nothing left for me, I lost a lot of money and I wanted to get a new house and car."

"You are really starting to piss me off, and if you don't get your ass in here now I'm going to come out and push you the fuck off!"

Nikki hit Luca on the arm, "Luca what's wrong with you, that won't help!"

Luca was losing his patience so he decided to think like a gambler, the other thing he hates more than drugs!

"Vin, how much did you lose?"

"Three hundred grand!" Luca bit his tongue, turning away to curse under his breath, "what a fucking idiot, when he gets in here I'm going to kill him myself."

"Ok listen I was going to tell you this tomorrow but I think now would be a good time, I got this huge tip on a horse so you can make it up."

"Really? You got a tip?"

"Of course, it's a sure win. So come in and we can talk about it."

Vinny looked at Luca and smiled; "really?"

Luca smiled back, "Yeah, now get your ass inside because I'm freezing."

Vinny finally got back into the room and once he was safe inside Luca smacked him across the head, "what the fuck are you thinking getting on the ledge and wanting to jump? For money? Are you kidding me, what made you think you couldn't come to me for help? Don't ever do that to me again, you are the closest thing I have for a brother and the last thing I want is to lose you. You ever gamble again I will break all of your fucking fingers! How many times do I have to tell you that shit is no good?"

Nikki just stared at Luca, "yeah that will lift his spirits, Vinny don't ever think in life that you have no other option, you have a great friend here who would bend over backwards for you."

Luca shot Nikki a distasteful look, "Okay babe, relax, I'm not bending over for no one!" Nikki let out a loud laugh, "NOT THAT! Vinny you know what I mean." She hugged him and kissed him on the cheek, "I like you too much to see anything bad happen to you."

Luca pulled her away from Vinny, "Yeah that's all good, no more hugging and kissing. Now Vinny tell me how much you need and we will fix this mess in the morning." Vinny thanked them both.

They walk back in their room and Luca walked towards the bed while Nikki stood by the door just staring at him. He was still going on, on how upset he was over Vinny. He turned around and just looked at her standing there, "what's wrong with you? Are you ok?"

Nikki now had a hot sexy smile on her face, "Babe you look so hot in your sweats and no shirt. Your body is amazing." He started to strut his stuff and show off his abs. Nikki couldn't help but laugh. She walked over to him and just kissed him.

He looked at her, "Babe it's been a long night and we have a flight to catch tomorrow so let's get some sleep." They both got in bed and fell asleep.

CHAPTER 21

BACK IN NEW YORK the goons, Mike and the chief were behind closed doors in the office discussing the events of the meeting. Joe started to explain to them that Luca was trying to turn the five families away from the drug business and into the entertainment business.

Mike was not too pleased about this. "This is not going the way we thought!"

Joe agreed with Mike; "You don't understand everything we have worked for is going down the tubes with these two fucking idiots!"

Paul tried to calm Joe down; "Joe you need to relax, this is just a bump in the road. We now have to step up and take action."

Joe looked at Mike, "You realize we have to get rid of the both of them?"

Mike looked at the chief and this was the last thing the chief wanted to do. "Listen guys we can't have blood on our hands, we are the FBI for God sake."

The guys all looked at each other and Joe finally smiled, having a revelation. "You're right and we don't have to. We will do what we said before; we will get pictures of Nikki and show them to Luca. He will see she is a Fed and he will have no choice but to get rid of her."

The chief looked at Joe, "That's great and all but Luca is so in love with Nikki, how can he get rid of her?"

Joe chuckled, "That's the whole point, he won't be able to and when he fails they will get rid of the both of them. That way we don't get our hands dirty." They all looked at each other and smiled.

The chief put his head down but at the same was happy about the plan. "Okay, so I'll get her here today and you guys get ready to snap some pictures. The shipment is coming in tonight and we need to move these drugs."

Paul nodded, "we have that under control, and you just keep the coast clear so we can move it." Everyone is in agreement.

* * * * *

NIKKI AND THE GUYS were in the car coming back from the airport. Everyone was exhausted from the night they had. Vinny couldn't stop apologizing to them for what had happened. Nikki was very understanding but Luca of course had to give Vinny a hard time. "I swear Vin you ever pull a stunt like that I will kill you myself." Vinny was lost for words. As they were in the car Nikki's phone rang. Looking at the caller ID and realized it was the chief. She turned the phone off.

Luca looked at her, "who was that?"

Nikki put her phone away, "it's my boss but I'll call him when I get home, I need to be up and awake to speak to him."

Luca just nodded and continued to suspect that it was someone else. "Are you sure?"

Nikki rolled her eyes, "yes Luca it's my boss." He looked away and continued to drive. Vinny was passed out in the back seat mumbling in his sleep.

They arrived at Nikki's place and said goodbye. "Listen I'll call you later Bianca, I have a few things to take care of today, you get some rest and take care of that stomach bug." Nikki smiled and walked up to her apartment. Once inside, she called the chief.

"Chief is everything Ok?"

"Yes everything is fine; I was wondering if maybe you can swing by, I wanted to discuss the meeting. Joe and Paul told me all about it."

"Joe and Paul?"

"Yes, the goons."

"Oh ok I didn't know their names, sure give me an hour and I will be down there."

"Sure thing, just give me a buzz when you are on your way."

Nikki agreed and hung up. Suddenly that queasy feeling in her stomach hit again, sending her racing to the bathroom to throw up. "What the heck is going on? I need to call my doctor and see if he can give me something for this." She took a quick shower and got dressed. She tried to eat a slice of toast but it didn't stay down. When she arrived at the headquarters, she found it really odd that the chief was outside waiting for her. She got out of her car and walked up to him, "Chief? You are waiting for me?" He smiled at her,

"I actually came down for a smoke."

"We have a smoking area inside."

"Yes I know, but I needed some air."

"Ok did you want to go inside and talk?"

"No, actually it's really quick, no need to go in plus Mike is up there and I know how much you two hate each other."

"Hate is such an understatement, but that's fine, what's up? Did the boys fill you in?"

"Yes, and from what I understand there is a huge shipment so we are going to take it from here."

"What do you mean? This is my investigation."

"Yes I know, but we don't want the risk of Luca seeing you."

"Well, Luca has nothing to do with this."

"I understand that Nikki but if he's there you know they will take him in."

"Fine you do what you have to and I will do what I have to." Nikki turned and walked away from the chief and started towards her car.

The chief yelled out to her, "Nikki you better not do anything stupid!"

Nikki just got into her car and drove away. While driving, she called Larry and tried to explain what went down.

"Larry listen to me we are going to this shipment."

"Nikki what are you planning? The chief said they are taking it from here."

"Yeah but Larry I have a really bad feeling. I just want to see what goes down and if Luca will be there."

"Nikki you know you can't do anything."

"I know but I just need to be there."

"Ok Nikki whatever you want. I'll meet you at the warehouse."

"Thanks Larry."

"Anytime, George and I will be there by ten o'clock."

Nikki ran home with a mission. She knew that Mike and the chief were up to no good and she was going to bring them down. She changed hurriedly and as she was ready to walk out the door Luca called her.

"Bianca what's going on, how are you feeling?"

Nikki didn't want Luca coming over tonight; she had plans to meet with Larry and George.

"I'm feeling a little better but I'm actually going to have some tea and head to bed."

"Really, are you getting sick of me already?"

"No, I'm just not feeling well and I don't want you to get you sick."

"You're right, that's actually a good idea. Get some rest and I will talk to you in the morning."

"Ok thanks, I love you."

"I love you too." Nikki turned the phone off, grabbed her bag and ran out.

Larry and George were waiting in the van outside the warehouse. The warehouse was in a secluded area behind the train tracks. As Nikki was going there she couldn't help but think that this place looked very familiar. She dismissed the thought and continued to the van. George opened the door, "Hey stranger long time no see."

Nikki smiled at George and looked over at Larry, "Did I miss anything?"

"No nothing, they are still waiting for a few guys. The goons are there and some of the guys from the Boston family. Nik, Luca isn't here."

She breathed a sigh of relief, "I didn't think he would be. He can't risk being caught. That would be a stupid move on his part. I doubt any of the bosses will be here just the spiders."

George looked at Nikki and noticed something different about her, "Nikki are you ok, you seem a little off?"

"Why do you say that?"

"I don't know you just have a different look about you."

"Well you haven't really seen me, and I've been sick, I have a stomach bug and haven't been myself the last few days."

"Well you better cough the other way because I don't want to get sick." Nikki just smiled.

"You see what I mean; you are not even fighting with me."

"George no offence, but I'm not in the mood I'm not feeling well."

Larry interrupted them, "Everyone is here."

Nikki looked around to see if there were any unmarked police cars around but saw nothing but old trains and containers. "If the feds are making this bust, where is everyone?"

George just shrugged his shoulder, "Honestly I don't think there will be a bust."

Nikki was furious, the chief played her like a fiddle and she was going to get even. They stuck around until everyone was gone, and everything was taken away. No feds, No bust! "Larry first thing in the morning I'm going to meet with internal affair, if you want you can come, or I can simply go alone."

Larry looked at George and then back at Nikki, "No Nik, we got your back."

She was glad to hear that. She got in her car and went home.

CHAPTER 22

NIKKI AND THE BOYS were waiting patiently outside the office. Larry saw that Nikki is looking really pale in the face, "Nikki relax it's going to be ok."

She just smiled and nodded. Mary Winters came out to greet the three of them. She was a very tall woman, not that easy on the eyes but she was a woman and Nikki thought *maybe it's a good thing.*

"Nikki Jacobs?"

"Yes." Nikki and the boys get up, she mumbled under breath, "let me do all the talking."

"Please come in and have a seat. What can I do for you?"

"As you know I've been working on the Marchiosio case."

"Yes we have been aware of that."

"Well a lot of things have been happening that makes me thing that a few of our men are somehow involved in some kind of conspiracy."

"Ms. Jacobs you realize this is a serious accusation? You are talking about the department."

"Yes, I understand completely, but I have given the Chief plenty of evidence and chances to make busts on shipments that have come in and no busts have been made."

"What exactly do you believe is going on?"

"I think the department is using the drugs and recycling it. Selling it to the families and making money. For example, the huge busts we made from Colombia with Emilio Escobar, all those drugs that we took in were later gone. They were selling them to the mob and making a profit for themselves."

"Nikki listen this is some real strong accusations and you need to have some major proof to back you up."

"The drugs are all gone, they sold them."

"Can you prove that?" Nikki stood in silence and looked at her boys. "Listen all I'm asking is to just start and investigation and look into it. Yesterday a huge shipment came in from South America and the Chief told me he was on it and making the bust. We camped out last night and nothing was done. I don't know what they are doing but all I'm asking is to look into."

"Listen Nikki I'm sorry you had to waste your time to come in but unless you have some hard proof we can't just assume." Nikki was getting really frustrated; at this point she thought everyone was in on it. She got up and looked at Mrs. Winter dead in the face, "FINE I guess I will have to go out there and prove to you that I am right! Thanks for your time, have a nice day." The boys got up and followed Nikki out. Mrs. Winter saw the determination in Nikki's eyes and was afraid that she was going to get herself killed. She made a quick call and just looked at Nikki and shook her head.

Nikki was pissed. Larry tried to calm her down but there was no getting through to her. "I can't fucking believe this! Are we the only three fucking idiots that are not in this?"

Larry had some news but was really nervous to tell Nikki, he knew this would put her over the edge but he was her friend and wanted to let her in on what he had heard. "Nikki I'm going to tell you something but you have to promise me that you will not lose it.   It's something I heard, and right now it's just hearsay."

She just gave him a look, "Larry can it really get any worse than this?"

He just raised his eyebrows and hoped for the best. "They are looking to bust Luca on narcotics, prostitution and gambling."

"WHAT, ARE YOU FUCKING KIDDING ME?"

"I heard it last night and I didn't want to tell you but I thought that you needed to hear this."

"NARCOTICS,   PROSTITUION,   AND GAMBLING, LUCA?"   OH MY GOD, THE MAN CAN'T STAND GAMBLING! HE NEVER GAMBLED A DAY IN HIS LIFE!"

"They are just throwing things out there; you know how they get when they can't pin anything on someone, they start throwing shit in the wind."

"This is so wrong! The FBI is worse than the mob I am so convinced. I'm sure they even killed people! I promise you this Larry before they even try to get Luca back in prison I will have them all locked up!"

Larry knew it was a bad idea telling her, "Listen just go home and take care of your bug and I will keep you posted. Please you need to just rest."

Nikki just looked at Larry and he could see in her eyes that she needed the rest. The last couple of days had been very stressful on her.

"Thanks Larry I will try and please anything you hear, you better call me!" Larry just nodded and she left.

CHAPTER 23

THE GOONS CALLED A private meeting with the five families but Luca wasn't part of that it. They had information that they felt that had to be shared with the families. Joe stood up and started the meeting. "First of all I want to thank everyone for meeting us on short notice but it's come to our attention that someone among is working with Feds." Everyone looked at each other and was wondering which one of them was the rat. "No it's no one here. We have evidence that Bianca, Luca's girlfriend is working as an undercover fed." All the men in the room started to whisper among themselves.

Carlo was the first to chuckle, "yeah I knew she wasn't who she said she was; how did you find this out?"

Paul pulled out the pictures of Nikki and Chief and passed them around the table. "We also knew she wasn't who she said she was so we tailed her and lo and behold. As you can see she is in front of the headquarters talking to the chief. Now I don't think Luca knows but Luca is so in love with her that we believe he tells her more than he should. We don't need her snooping around. She can take us all down."

Peter Russo the older boss and the most respected gave Bianca the benefit of the doubt. He really liked Luca and didn't want to cast the first stone, "if this is true then why didn't they make a bust last night? That would've been the perfect opportunity."

The goons looked at each other and Joe stood up, "we thought the same thing and the only thing we could've came up with was that he didn't mention this to her but we can't take a chance. We decided we need to stop all shipments until this problem is taken care of." Mikey looked at them, "what do you suggest we do, take out a fed?"

Joe responded, "What other choice do we have?"

Mikey smirked, "well I honestly don't want that blood on my hands." Everyone looked at each other in agreement; they knew that if they got caught they would be put away for life. Joe continued to tell them the plan, "well we thought that too and yes, no one wants that blood on their hands so we thought maybe Luca should get this information and take care of it." The old man couldn't believe his ears, "you want Luca to take out the woman that he loves?" Joe smiled, a sinister gleam was in his eyes, "well he brought her in and should be the one to take her out."

"But he is in love with her."

"He took an oath to the family and he has to do right by the family, and if this means taking care of the problem then he has to do it." Everyone looked at each other in agreement. Peter put his head down, "I'll tell him, give me the pictures. I will meet with Luca and tell him what has to be done. We can't have this and as much as it's going to kill Luca he has to take care of it."

Joe handed the pictures to Peter, "Great, thanks. Once we have confirmation that this has been done then we can proceed with our business in the meantime boys be careful what you say because you don't know who's been bugged." They all stood up and thanked the goons.

Mr. Russo wasn't too happy to deliver the news but he knew that this matter had to be taken care of.

∗ ∗ ∗ ∗ ∗

THE NEXT MORNING LUCA walked into the Café and sat down next to Peter Russo. They exchange hellos. Luca could see that something was bothering the old man.

"Peter is everything ok; you seemed a little tense this morning on the phone."

"Luca last night we had a meeting with the Canadian boys."

"A meeting, without me?"

"A serious matter was brought to our attention and it's something that you need to see for yourself." Mr. Russo slid the pictures over to Luca.

Luca grabs the pictures and saw Bianca and the chief in front of the FBI headquarters. He looked at the old man, puzzled.

"Peter what is this all about?"

"That's Bianca with the Chief of the FBI. Bianca is an undercover fed and you are her subject. Now before you start, you need to know that I tried really hard to give her the benefit of the doubt, but as you know this not a joking matter. The families were not too pleased about this and how a fed got on the inside. What we do, we work hard to keep quiet and to have a fed come in so easy made the families a little worried."

Luca was dying inside. He just kept staring at the pictures and couldn't believe his eyes. His world has just been torn apart. The woman that he loved more than life itself was a rat and he hated rats more than anything.

Peter saw that Luca wasn't taking this too well. "Luca listen I know this will be hard to hear, but this matter needs to be taken care of. The families want to get rid of Bianca and if you can't do it I will have someone else take care of it. They feel you brought her in, you should be the one to take her out."

Luca looked up at the old man with a stone cold face, "No, this is my problem and I will take care of it. I will do what I have to do for the family."

Peter let out a sigh, "I know this is going to be hard but Luca you have to understand that if you don't take care of this, they are going to take matters in their own hands and come after you."

Luca looked at the picture again, "No I will do it tonight, and I hate rats!"

They both stood up and Peter hugged Luca, "I'm sorry about this Luca but it has to be like this." Luca just nodded and walked out.

He sat in the car just staring at the pictures. He didn't know if he wanted to scream or just beat the fuck out of somebody. The emotions that were churning inside were too intense to describe. The pain of betrayal for Luca was the worst thing in the world. He loved her so much he didn't understand how this could happen. At the same time he was so mad at himself for letting a woman break him this way. How could he let his guard down and disappoint the families like this? He was fighting with himself, "If she was here I swear I would crush her like a grape but at the same time kiss her and never let her go." He hit the steering wheel so hard that he hurt his hand. He was furious but he knew he had to this. He picked up the phone and called her. "Bianca, what's going on?"

She was very happy to hear his voice, she was having the morning from hell and the only person she could think about was him. "Luca I miss you today and I'm so glad to hear your voice." At this point he didn't believe anything that came out of her mouth, he didn't trust her and in his eyes she was nothing but a rat!

He tried to be as normal as possible but he came off very cold and distant. "Really you miss me?"

Nikki noticed he was off and became very defensive, "What's wrong with you, why are you so cold?"

Luca took control of himself, "Oh no babe I had a lonely night without you last night and I woke up a little cranky but I was hoping that maybe we can make it up tonight. You think I can pick you up later and we can go for ride?"

Nikki smiled and couldn't wait to see him; she had so much to tell him but didn't know where to start, "yes, I would love to see you later."

Luca just held the phone in his hand and just wanted to bang it on the dash board, "Ok so I'll pick you up later."

She said to him, "I Love you Luca." He couldn't say it back and just hung up. She just looked at the phone and was mad that he didn't say it back. She thought *maybe he had a bad day just like I did. It's fine. I'll see him later and we'll make up the lost time.*

* * * * *

NIKKI TOOK A LONG nap and was woken up by the ringing of the phone. She jumped up and realized she slept the day away. "Hello?"

Luca was on the other end, "Bianca it's me, I should be there in a half hour."

She rubbed her eyes and looked at the time; it was seven thirty, "Oh wow I slept the day away. Luca give me an hour. I'm just waking up and need to shower and get ready."

He wasn't himself, "Sure see you then." He just hung up with no goodbyes or I love you. He wasn't even calling her babe anymore. Nikki found this very strange but she'd been having a strange two days so she just brushed it off. She got herself in the shower then got ready. Luca would be there soon and she was just very excited to see him. She finished earlier than she anticipated, so she sat on the couch to catch on the current events. She couldn't help but drift away and think about the events of the last few months. She was very happy to have met Luca and she realized how much her life has changed and the changes that soon would take place. She was in deep thought when she was jolted back to the present with an ear shattering clap of thunder from outside. The weather was horrible; it was raining, thundering and lighting. Nikki looked at the time and noticed that Luca was late, "it's not like him to be late." After a good twenty minutes there was a knock on the door. She jumped off the couch and opened the door. Luca was standing there and every bit of hate that he had for her earlier vanished. She was a vision and he couldn't help but hug her and kiss her. He loved her so much and hated what he had to do. She had him come in while she grabbed her jacket and bag. Luca was very quiet and just watched her. She asked what was wrong but he didn't really talk. She looked out the window, "are you sure you don't want to just stay inside, it's horrible out there."

He shook his head, "No I want to go for a ride."

She grabbed her bag, "Ok then let's go I'm ready."

The rain was really coming down outside but inside the car it was very quiet. Nikki tried to start a conversation but Luca was just not into talking. His head was all over the place. He tried to think back and figure out how he didn't pick it up. He did recall the one time she started to ask a lot of questions and he asked her if she was fed and her reply was sarcastic, *"yes and part of my job is to fuck you."* Why didn't he see it then? How did he let that go? He was so blinded by her that he let his guard down, and he was so mad at himself for falling right into her trap. The questions just kept going through his head, did she really love him? Was everything a big lie? Was this love one sided? He was beating himself up quietly and she noticed that something was bothering him.

"Luca what's wrong, is everything ok?"

He looked at her, "yeah I just had a bad day." She touched his leg as he was driving, "do you want to talk about it?"

He looked at her hand and back into her eyes, "No."

Nikki accepted that and just looked out the window. It was dreary and wet. They stopped by the train tracks and the bar came down as a train was about to pass. She suddenly got a sick feeling in her stomach. The rain, the lighting, the train, she thought of her dream and she just shot a look at Luca, "where are we going?"

He just kept looking straight, "just for a ride."

She touched her stomach, "I don't feel so well."

He didn't respond, the bar came up and he continued to drive. She just kept looking out the window. They came up to a dead end road and Luca stopped the car. She couldn't see anything but rain, dirt and trees. "Luca where are we, what are we doing here?"

Luca touched his side and made sure his piece was there. He felt sick to his stomach, *how can I kill the woman I love?* Nikki was getting frustrated with the silent treatment and the one word answers, "Luca what the fuck is going on?"

He looked at her, "Come on get out let's take a walk."

Nikki looked outside, "Hello, do you not see the pouring rain?"

Luca just walked out of the car. Nikki mumbled under her breath, opened the door and walked out after him. "Luca you are making me nervous, what's wrong?

Tell me what happened, I have never seen you like this and I don't like it."

He turned around and said, "You have NO IDEA the day I'm having."

Nikki stopped and grabbed his arm to stop him, "So why don't you tell me?"

Luca pulled away from her and she just stood there with her mouth open. "What the fuck is your problem?"

They were standing in the rain, both soaked to the skin now. They saw a daylight bright flash of lightning followed by ear shattering, loud thunder. Luca looked up the sky. "I found out some stuff today that killed me. They should've just killed me it would've hurt a lot less, it would've been easier not to feel the pain I'm feeling now."

Nikki stared at him with a confused expression and stepped closer to him. "Luca there's something I need to tell you, and I really don't know how you are going to take it." He pulled away and put his hand on his piece, "what is it?"

Nikki was just about to speak when started to get really sick and throws up. She was bent over and he was over her thinking, *this is the best time to do it, just pull the trigger she won't know what hit her*. He went for his piece but stopped himself, *I can't do it, I just can't*. He leaned over her, "are you still sick, are you okay?"

She straightened up, still coughing, "I'm okay. It's actually want I wanted to talk to you about. This afternoon before I passed out for a nap I got sick. I was going to call the doctor but then I realized that I was late on my period, so I decided to take a test instead and it was positive." Luca was speechless; he didn't know what to say.

"Bianca what are you saying?"

"Luca, I'm pregnant." Luca didn't know what to do or say. His emotions were on a roller coaster ride. Not only did he have to kill the woman he loved but now she was having his child!

"Bianca, are you kidding me?"

Nikki was confused she couldn't read him at all, "No I'm not; I took the test twice."

How am I supposed to kill her now? She was carrying my child. He thought that this was an answer from God; he loved her so much that he didn't have it in him to kill her and now that she's pregnant, he couldn't do it. He wrapped his arms around her, "Let's get you back in the car."

CHAPTER 24

LUCA WALKED INTO the café and sat down next to Vinny. He seemed stressed and disconnected, and Vinny just sat there watching him fidgeting.

"Luca are you ok, what's going on?"

"Vin the families want me dead, they are going to come after me?"

"What are you talking about? Luca what the fuck did you do?"

"I'm thinking if I can take them all out first, then I don't have to run."

"Luca how many times do I have to tell you to stop watching *The Godfather?* It's a fucking movie; it's not really like that. That's all Hollywood. What the fuck are you smoking?"

"Vin you have to promise me one thing, if something happens to me, promise me that you will take care of Bianca for me."

"Luca you are talking in riddles and you are starting to scare the shit out of me, what the fuck is going on?"

Just as he was about to tell Vinny what was going on, Carlo, Louie, Peter and Mikey walked in. They said hello to everyone and walk over to Luca and Vinny.

Peter has his hand on Luca's shoulder, "Luca my boy, how are you today?" Luca couldn't look at him in the eye, "Gentlemen why don't you have a seat, Tony bring the guys espresso." They sit down and Peter looks at

Luca again, "Luca did you take care of what you were supposed to last night?"

Luca put his eyes down, "No actually I didn't, something came up and I couldn't do it last night, but don't worry I will take care of it soon."

Carlo took a sip of his espresso, "You know Luca we can't do any business until this matter is taken care of."

Luca was not too fond of Carlo and looked at him straight in the face, "don't worry your pretty little head Carlo, if I say I'm going to take care of it, I'm going to take care of it. After all I am the one who took the rap for the last four years. I didn't see anyone else stepping up. So don't worry, if anyone has true devotion and dedication to the families it's me." Carlo felt his face turn beat red because Luca put him in his place. He knew that four years ago no one stepped up, but he still didn't have to like Luca.

Louie interrupted the both of them, "with all due respect we have a business to run here and unless you do something quick, we have to take matters in our own hands."

Luca looked stone-faced at the men, "I will take care of it."

Carlo and the boys looked at each other. They got up and said their goodbyes.

Peter pulled Luca over, "Luca I told you yesterday that if you can't do it we can get someone to take care of it. Now you know that this is out of my hands and I can't protect you." Luca nodded, appreciating the respect that the old man was showing him, "I know Peter and I thank you very much but this is something that I have to do myself." Luca hugged him and told him to keep in touch. The other men waited for the old man by the door, Carlo got close to Peter, "you know we have to do, what we have to do."

Peter nodded in disappointment.

Vinny, sitting across from Luca just continued to stare at him as Luca continuously stirred his coffee. Vinny looked away released a sigh then looked back at Luca. "So are you going to tell me what the fuck just happened?"

Luca didn't look up. He just kept looking at his espresso.

"They are going to kill me Vinny."

"WHY, what did you do?"

"It's more like what didn't I do." He finally looked up at Vinny and looks at him straight in the face, "Bianca is an undercover Fed and I was her subject."

"I KNEW IT! She was way too hot to just hook up with you."

"Vin, really? You see I'm already down. You want to keep kicking me even more? Anyway, those two assholes from Canada tailed her and they took some pictures of her with the chief. Now you know how much I hate rats, so I had to take care of her."

Vinny got closer to Luca and whispered, "YOU FUCKING GOT RID OF BIANCA?"

Luca looked down and Vinny could see he was really hurting, "I was supposed to, I couldn't do it Vin, I couldn't fucking do it!"

Vinny straightened out and put his hands through his hair, "what the fuck Luc, what are you going to do?"

Luca just stared up the ceiling, "Vin, I feel so betrayed and I swear I was going to put a bullet through her even though it was killing me, but then she told me."

Vinny got closer again, "She told you she was a fed and she decided to give it all up because she loves you and you are the only man for her?"

Luca did a double take, looking at Vinny, "Yo Vin do me a favor, when you're home and have nothing to do don't watch fucking soap operas, put on *The Godfather!* NO, she told me that she's pregnant."

Vinny just covered his face, "Shit Luca, now I see your problem, so what's the plan, what do you want me to do?"

Luca smiled, "you're a great friend Vin, I don't want you to get involved, then they'll come after you." Vinny got mad.

"How can you say that? We are brothers. I always have your back. Now tell me, what's the plan?"

"Okay honestly, I just want you to watch over Bianca. If you can, go get her today at the apartment and take her to safe place. I just want her to be safe; I'll deal with the boys."

"Luca I have one question."

"What is it?"

"Why didn't you tell the boys she was pregnant, I'm sure they would've understood."

"Vin she's a Fed, they are not letting her go. I'd rather take the bullet for her even if she wasn't pregnant."

"Luca, she's a rat you would do that?"

"Vin I love her."

"Luca I never seen you like this before."

"Listen, just go and get Bianca and keep me posted. I don't want them seeing us together because then they will take us both out."

Vinny got up and gave Luca a hug, "I don't know how much this means but congratulations on the baby."

Luca smiled, "thanks bro that means a lot to me coming from you."

*   *   *   *   *

VINNY ARRIVED AT BIANCA'S place and knocked on the door a few times. He started to get really frustrated because she was not answering. He called her cell but it went directly to voice mail. At this point Vinny was getting really nervous that someone got here before him. He went downstairs and asked the doorman if he's seen Bianca, the doorman doesn't know Bianca. Then Vinny realizes that that's not her real name so he asks if he's seen the women from apartment 4A.

"Oh Nikki, no she left last night and I haven't seen her since." Vinny was now scared that something happened to her. How was he going to explain to Luca that she was nowhere to be found? "Did she leave with anyone?"

The guy thought back, "yes, she left with the man who is always here, Luca something." Vinny thanked the guy and left. He thought to himself, *Luca was with her last night but he did drop her off, so where the heck did she go?*

* * * * *

LUCA WENT TO SEE Mr. B. He felt he owed it to him to explain what was going on; after all Mr. B was a father figure to him.

Mr. B was very happy to see Luca; he hugged him and asked him to sit down. "Luca, what's going on? Why am I hearing these rumours, tell me they are just rumours."

Luca shook his head, "No Mr. B they are all true, I was just as shocked as you. I really don't know how I messed up like this. It's not like me to drop my guard and have a rat get into the family."

"Tell me you took care of it?"

"I went to take care of it last night but things came up and I couldn't go through with it. I fell in love with a Fed Mr. B., how did this happen?"

"Luca women have a way of putting you under their spell, look at Adam and Eve. Listen, I know this is hard and you love her, but Luca she's a fed and you know the families are going to take matters in their own hands."

"Yeah I know and I'm willing to accept any consequences, but there's something I need to tell you, Mr. B. She's having my baby."

"Is this why you couldn't go through with it?"

"Honestly I don't know what I was going to do, Mr. B I will take the bullet for her and my child, but I need them to be protected."

"Luca you are like a son to me and the only advice I can give you is, do what you know is right."

"Thanks Mr. B." The men got up and Mr. B hugged Luca, "Take care Luca and please be careful."

Luca nodded, "I will, thank you."

Just as he was leaving his phone rang.

"Hello?"

"Luca I can't find her anywhere."

"What are you talking about; she's not in her apartment?"

"No, I even asked the doorman and he said he saw her leave with you last night."

"But I drove her back; did you ask if he saw anyone waiting for her?"

"He doesn't work the night shift; I have to wait for the guy at night."

"FUCK! They got her. Vin just stay by her place and see if she gets back or if you see anyone snooping around. I will go look for her."

Luca didn't know where to look first. He had all these bad thoughts whirling around in his head *where she can be? They got to her, she's dead!* The thought in his head that she was dead was breaking him apart, he couldn't breathe. "She can't be dead, I still feel her. FUCK BIANCA WHERE ARE YOU?" He was driving like a crazy man. He kept touching base with Vinny and he didn't hear anything either. He even called some of the guys to try to get information, but they had no clue on what was going on.

As he was driving around he got a call from Carlo, "Luca listen tonight we are having a meeting by the old warehouse in Brooklyn, you need to be there."

Luca wanted to ask him where Bianca was but he had a feeling that that was what the meeting was about. He thought *they have her and they are going to kill her in front of me.* "Sure Carlo no problem I'll see you tonight." He called Vinny and told him about the meeting but he wanted Vinny to stay away, watch her apartment just in case. Vinny hesitated, "Luca please don't go, or let me go with you."

Luca shut him up, "NO I have to go and I don't want you there."

Vinny knew this meeting wasn't going to be good. "Fine, Luca please be careful."

Luca was quiet for a while, "I will Bro thanks for everything." He hung up and knew that this was it for him.

CHAPTER 25

"WHY ARE YOU HOLDING me here and making me listen to all this?" Nikki was sitting in a room being detained against her own free will. "This is so wrong in every level. He is going crazy looking for me; can I please just call him and tell him I'm ok?" She was getting really frustrated, "If you don't let me he will end up doing something stupid and get himself killed." She was in tears and she couldn't believe he knew who she was and that he was going to kill her last night. She touched her belly and tears just kept rolling down her face. She didn't care for the investigation anymore; all she wanted was Luca, the father of her unborn child. She loved him so much that she was willing to throw the whole investigation out the window. "Please I'm begging you, just one call."

The head of internal affairs looked around, "we are doing this to protect you. You came to us for help and we stepped in. Now he knows who you are and they want to kill you."

Nikki couldn't stop crying, "But they are going to kill him and he's one of the good guys." Mary Winters did feel for Nikki but she was doing it for her own good. Nikki knew where the old warehouse was and she had to get to Luca to warn him but she needed to get out of this office. "Ok well can I least go to the bathroom?"

Mary looked at her, "Of course, you are not a prisoner we are just protecting you."

Nikki got up, "Yes I know, thank you." Nikki got out of there so fast. They will find out soon enough but it gave her a head start. She ran to her car and got all soaked. It was pouring outside and she just looked up and started to realize that this was the dream she kept having. She got into the car and took off. She must have blown every red light, but she didn't care. All she kept thinking about was her Luca, and how much she loved him. They had him bugged so she heard everything he said today and she couldn't believe how the two goons and the chief set her up like that. She was glad that Internal Affairs got involved but now she feared for Luca's life. She tried calling Luca but the weather was so bad that nothing was going through. She also tried Vinny but the same thing; she kept getting a dead zone. She got to the part in her dream at the train track, she prayed that the bar wouldn't come down but it did. She got out of the car and started to scream, "LUCA!" The warehouse was just past the tracks but she knew he couldn't hear her. She got back in the car and waited for the bar to go up.

* * * * *

LUCA WALKED INTO THE warehouse and said hello to everyone. He looked around hoping to see Bianca but she was nowhere to be seen. Carlo motioned for Luca to take a seat.

Luca refused, "It's Ok I'll stand." He looked around again, "Ok so where is she?" The boys looked at each other and Carlo looked back at Luca.

"What are you talking about?"

"I know you have her so where is she?"

"Luca we have no idea what you are talking about."

"BIANCA, WHAT DID YOU DO WITH BIANCA?"

"We were going to ask you the same thing."

"What do you mean?"

"Well we went looking for your precious Fed but she was nowhere to be found so we brought you here to find out where she is."

"I have been looking for her all day and I thought you guys already got to her."

"No, nobody got to anybody so why don't you stop playing the games and tell us where she is."

"Carlo I have been going crazy all day looking for her."

"Where's Vinny?"

"He's staking out in front of her place waiting to see if she gets back."

"So tell me Luca did you have any intentions of taking care of this problem?"

Just as Carlo finished his sentence, Nikki comes storming in screaming, "LUCA!" Everyone jumped from their seats with their guns in their hands.

Luca looks at Nikki, "Bianca what are you doing here?"

She ran to him kissed, and hugged him, "Luca I love you so much." Luca is so happy to see her alive but still very mad that she showed up. This is exactly what he didn't want to happen, both being there so the boys could take them both out.

"Bianca why didn't you stay away?"

She had tears in her eyes, "I couldn't, I couldn't lose you, I love you too much and I had to come and warn you."

Carlo smiled evilly and walked over to the both of them, "OH isn't this sweet? Just what I wanted; the both of you in front of me. Bianca, Nikki whatever your fucking name is, you just made our life a little easier. You see we couldn't find you but you found us."

Nikki let go of Luca and stares at Carlo in the face, "you stupid son of a bitch, I don't know who you think you are, but God help you if you touch him."

Carlo laughs at loud, "Oh my God is she for real? Luca where did you find her anyway, she's got spunk I like her. Too bad she's a fucking RAT!"

Luca saw one of the spiders getting ready with his gun; he knew that this was it. "Carlo I will rip you to shreds if you hurt her."

Carlo looked at Tony and gave him the "go ahead" look.

Tony pulled up his hand and lets out a shot. Luca all ready for this, jumped and knocked Nikki out of the way.

Nikki screams out just like in her dream, "LUCA NO!"

Just as Luca hit the floor, the door of the warehouse slammed open and the FBI screamed out; "FREEZE!"

Nikki just watched Luca hit the floor. In tears, she knelt on the floor and held a bleeding Luca in her arms, whispering in his ear, "Babe please don't leave me, I love you so much."

Carlo just glared at Nikki as the Feds came in and cuffed everyone, "I hope you're happy you stupid bitch!"

Nikki didn't even look up; she just kept holding Luca and wishing that he would just wake up. Larry walked over to Nikki to try to pry her off of Luca so they could take him but she refused to let go of the lifeless body. "Larry he can't be dead, please tell me he's alive."

Larry shook his head and knelt down next to her, "I'm so sorry Nikki, I really am but he's dead."

She hugged Luca's dead body so tight and she just kept kissing him. "I love you so much Babe, please just wake up."

Larry pulled her by the arm, "Nikki please let go, come with me don't do this to yourself."

She looked at him with red blood shot eyes, "I did this, I killed him the man that I love, I got him killed. I should've told him everything; I knew he was one of the good ones. Why didn't I tell him Larry, WHY?" She looked down at Luca and kissed him one last time, "I love you babe, always, forever and eternity!"

Larry helped her up and he hugged her, "I really am truly sorry." She just covered her face on his chest and cried all the way to the car. She watched, feeling a deep hole in her soul, as they took Luca away in the black body bag and she touched her stomach, "I will always love you."

Larry had orders to take Nikki straight to headquarters for questioning. She was just sitting in the interrogation room looking down at her blood stained hands and clothes. She had Luca's blood all over her and she was sick to her stomach. She couldn't breathe just with the thought that she was not going to see him, that her child would never know his father. She was just so numb and lifeless herself.

Mary Winters walked in and sits down. "Nikki you know we have a change of clothes if you want to wash up and clean up." Nikki didn't respond, she just looked at her hands and pictured Luca laying there bleeding. Mary continued to talk to her but Nikki didn't care to listen. "Nikki what you did tonight was wrong, you left without orders. You walked into a bust and almost got yourself killed."

Nikki stared up at her, hostile, "YOU DID THIS! YOU KILLED HIM! If you would've let me call him he wouldn't have gone down there!"

Mary looked at her straight in the face, "you asked for our help, we stepped in and we protected our own. What you uncovered was bigger than anything I've seen. Because the Chief and some of the boys from the department were involved, we have to throw away every piece of incriminating evidence we have on the five families."

Nikki looked at her, "what are you talking about?"

"We can't use any of it and they are all going to be released by the morning."

"What about the Chief and Mike?"

"They have been stripped of their duties and are being detained in the other room."

"What about those two fucking assholes? Where are they?"

"They are also in custody."

"Good! I hope they rot in hell, all of them!"

"Nikki listen to me, what you did was huge and because of you we closed a long pending investigation."

"What are you saying? When I came to you, you looked at me like I was crazy but in the meantime you knew all along that something was up? I should fucking kill you right here and now you stupid BITCH!"

"Nikki you are out of line! You are working with gangsters' way too long and you need to just calm down and relax!"

"RELAX? You killed the man that I love, the father of my child, HOW THE FUCK DO YOU EXPECT ME TO RELAX?"

"You are a very good agent, one of the best and the one mistake you made was to get to close to your subject. I'm sorry for what happened but you got too close."

"Not only is Luca dead, but everything I worked hard to do was all a waste because they are all getting off because the FBI is more corrupt then the mob, how ironic is that!"

Mary looked down at all the evidence on her desk, then gives the file back to Nikki, "I'm really sorry Nikki. You are free to go." She motioned for Larry to come in, "Can you please take agent Jacobs home."

Larry nodded and helped Nikki up. Nikki looked over at Mary, "if you knew then why didn't you stop it, why did it have to go this far?" Ms. Winters just motioned Larry to take her home.

The whole car ride Nikki was very quiet. Larry wanted to speak but he knew that she wouldn't respond. They arrived at her place and Larry just looked over at Nikki, "I'm sorry Nikki, if there's anything I can do for you, please do not hesitate to call."

Nikki just nodded and gave Larry a big hug, "Thanks for everything Larry; at least I can still trust you." She walked out and went into her building.

As she was waiting for the elevator Vinny came storming in, "Bianca, are you ok?"

She turned to look at him, just threw her arms around him and started to cry. "Vin, he's dead, Luca is dead."

Vinny already had gotten the news from Mr. B but he made a promise to his best friend that he would be there for Nikki and the baby. "I know Bianca, I know. Let's go upstairs and get you clean up."

Nikki looked at Vinny, "Vin, you can call me Nikki, that is my name."

Vinny looked at her in the eyes, "Yeah but my buddy loved your name Bianca and if you don't mind, I would like to continue to call you that."

Nikki actually smiled for the first time, "Sure Vin, but just you are allowed to call me that." She realized why Luca loved Vinny so much.

CHAPTER 26

As THE MONTHS PASSED Nikki tried really hard to move on but she thought of Luca every second of the day. At times she felt she couldn't breathe and needed to be in his arms. She was happy to be carrying his child; that she had a piece of Luca. There would be days where she would just stay in bed and cry all day. She would think back on the days she had with him and how much he changed her life. She never loved anyone the way she loved Luca. She tried to get distracted and started to take pictures again. She even went to Boston and took pictures of the places they went together. She couldn't go horseback riding because she was pregnant, but she would go to the track just to sit there and watch the horses. She missed him so much that she would cook his favorite dishes and set a plate just for him.

One day as usual she was drifting and thinking of him when she heard a knock on the door. She got up and opened the door.

Vinny was glad to see her showered and dressed. He had been really worried about her, especially since she was pregnant. He had promised his friend that he would be there for her and he didn't back down on his word.

He lifted the bag in his hand, "I figured you can use some company and brought you your favorite, Sushi." She looked at him and a tear formed in the corner of her eye. Vinny wanted to kick himself in the ass, "No Bianca I didn't mean to get you upset, I just really wanted to cheer you up."

Nikki smiled and hugged him, "Thank you Vinny you have been so great to me and I truly appreciate it, if it wasn't for you being here I would've totally lost it. I was actually craving sushi so I'm glad you brought it." She could see the look of relief in Vinny's face.

"How are you feeling Bianca, did you go to the doctor's today?"

"Yes as a matter of fact I have something to show you." She walked over to the fridge and got the sonogram picture off the fridge; she walked over and handed it to Vinny like a proud mom. "Isn't he cute, he has Luca's nose."

Vinny looked at the picture and smiled at Nikki, "How can you tell, he still looks like an alien BUT a very cute one." They both laughed. Nikki was a little over four months already, she wasn't really showing but her morning sickness finally had gone away. Vinny was a proud uncle, "Bianca I can't wait to meet him. You know I miss Luca very much and I'm very glad we have each other, and now we get a piece of Luca in your baby." Nikki smiled as she was setting table with Vinny. They both sat down and started to eat. Vinny felt her pain because he felt it too.

"Nikki you know I went to see Mr. B today."

"Oh really, how is he?

"He's doing better thank God. He had some great news." Nikki continued to eat and looked up at him. "He told me that the charges against the families have been dropped because of the conspiracy with the FBI. The agents that were involved are actually getting charged and put away."

"Good! I hope they rot in jail. I'm glad to hear that you won't be going to jail, I don't know what I would do if I lost you too. You and this baby are all I have left of Luca."

"I will not be going anywhere anytime soon. Actually Mr. B would like for you to come to the house this Sunday. The families are getting together and they want to extend their gratitude to you. They consider you a hero, how you exposed the FBI and how you got them all off."

"Well I did quit the bureau and looking for a new profession, maybe I can take over where Luca left off?" She let out a loud laugh. "Vinny that's nice, but I don't know if I 'm comfortable meeting with them, they killed Luca and I don't know if I can face Carlo."

"Listen I know how you feel but you have to come to peace with it. You have to eventually face them and maybe you can finally move on. It took me a while too, but I promise Bianca, it will get better." Nikki had tears in her eyes; she knew Vinny was right and that she had to eventually move on for the sake of the baby.

Vinny handed her an entertainment magazine, "Oh I forgot to show you this." She looked at it and smiled, "Vinny he was such a handsome man." On the cover was a picture of Luca in the movie "Mulberry to Rome", it was coming out next week and at least he had the chance to finish that and she would be able to see him. The book signing and the premiere were on the same night, she had to go. "Vinny I don't know if I can go to the premier and watch this."

Vinny let out a sigh, "I know what you mean, I don't know if I can go but at least we will be there together." She smiled and nodded. "So Bianca what do you say, you want to come this Sunday to Mr. B for Sunday dinner?" She looked at him and finally said yes. Vinny was very happy to hear that, "You know it will get you out of the house and you get to be with Luca's family." Vinny hung around after dinner and they watched one of Luca's favorite movie together, *The Godfather*. They sat there and just held each other and every part of the movie they would talk about how much Luca loved it and how much they missed him. She was happy to have Vinny and Vinny was happy to have her.

* * * * *

THE DAYS FELT REALLY long for Nikki but Sunday came pretty fast. She was in the car with Vinny heading to Mr. B's house, she was there before but now she was a little a nervous. She didn't know how she would react when she saw Carlo. She wasn't too happy with him at the funeral and she had a hard time accepting his apology. She hasn't seen them for a while and she didn't know how to act when she did see them. She didn't want to get out of the car.

Vinny opened the door, "Bianca you will do fine, come on Mrs. B made everything and anything you can eat. She is so excited to see you. You can't disappoint Mrs. B." Vinny always made everything look better than they were. He convinced her and she finally got out. They were greeted by Mrs. B. She was very excited to see Bianca. She hugged her and kissed her. "Bianca I am so happy that you accepted the invite. We loved Luca very much and you are now part of the family, so you are welcomed here anytime." She asked her how she was feeling and how the pregnancy was going. Nikki felt very welcomed and very happy to be treated like family.

"I'm doing better, thank you for having me."

"Nonsense, like I said you are family and always welcomed. Can I get you something to drink or eat?"

"No, I'm ok for now I'll wait for everyone."

"Vinny take her to the office. The boys are in there waiting." She grabbed her face and kissed her cheeks, "Bianca I am so happy Luca found you, you were the best thing in his life." They both hugged each other.

"He was the best thing in my life." She touched her stomach, "and I'm so glad I will always have him in my life."

Vinny walked Nikki into the office and the men all stood up and greeted them, Carlo, Peter, Mikey, Louie and Mr. B. Mr. B hugged Bianca and kissed her, "I'm so glad you came here today. How are you feeling? You know I consider the baby like my own grandson."

Nikki smiled, "yes Luca told me how you were a father figure for him and how much he loved you."

Carlo interrupted, "Bianca we asked you here because we are very grateful to you; the way you went out of your way for the family and uncovered the conspiracy. Who knew that the Feds were worse than the mob?"

Nikki just grinned, "You can call me Nikki." She thought to herself that only Luca and Vinny were allowed to call her that.

Carlo smiled, "well Nikki I speak for all of the families when I say we consider you a hero. We want you to know that if there's anything you need, anything at all we are here for you. You are now considered family, even though you are a Fed."

Vinny interrupted, "She no longer works for the FBI."

Nikki looked at Vinny and smiled, "Yeah, I realized it's safer to work for the mob, so if you guys have positions available?"

The boys let out a huge laugh and Peter put his arm around Nikki, "I see what Luca saw in you. We really do appreciate all your work and of course when the baby is born, we will consider him one of ours. After all you are having Luca's son." Nikki looked at them all, "thank you guys, it's really nice to know that you will be there and I appreciate it but I'm good."

Mrs. B came in, "I hate to interrupt but dinner is ready, and this pregnant woman has to feed a baby, so let's go eat and let's go celebrate Luca's life."

They all walked out and Mr. B held Nikki back, "Nikki, Luca loved you very much and I want you to know that when the family told him they had to get rid of you, he didn't want to. He was very distraught and very upset, now I see why. You are truly everything he ever wanted. I am glad he met you." He kissed her on the cheek.

"Thank you Mr. B. Luca spoke very highly of you and loved you very much too and I too see why."

They hugged each other, "come on let's get some food, Luca would be upset if he knew we weren't feeding his son." They walked into the dining room and had a great Sunday dinner. Nikki was actually happy she came, she saw from Luca's point of view why she loved them so much. They were friendly, welcoming and very loving. She rubbed her belly and just thought how great it would've been if Luca was sitting next her. On the ride back to her place she thanked Vinny for convincing her to go. She felt Luca just by being around his family.

Vinny smiled, "I miss him too."

CHAPTER 27

NIKKI WAS VERY HAPPY and upset all in one, today was the premiere and book signing for Mulberry to Rome. She couldn't wait to see Luca on the big screen but at the same time she was nervous on how she would feel seeing him and how much she would miss him. Vinny came to pick her up.

"You look great Bianca."

"Thanks but Vin I really don't think it's a good idea to go; I'm afraid it will only make me feel worse."

"Just think you will see him at his best, you will do fine and I will be there the whole time holding your hand."

"Ok. So the movie is first and then the book signing right after?"

"Yes, we don't have to go to the book signing if you don't want to."

"No I do, it's where me and Luca met."

"Are you ready to go?" Nikki took a long deep breath and said, "yes."

They arrived at the theatre and Mark the producer went straight up to Nikki and Vinny.

He kissed her hello, "Nikki I'm so happy you made it, you are really going to love it."

Nikki looked at Vinny and back at Mark, "I wouldn't have missed it for the world."

Mark escorted them both in, "I want you to sit next to me."

The movie started and Vinny and Nikki just looked at each other and held hands, they were ready to see the man in their life that they missed so much. Most of the movie Nikki was laughing and thinking what a great job Luca did, she really enjoyed it. By the end of the movie she was crying, she could never get enough of Luca. Mark gave her a DVD so she would have it and watch it whenever she wanted.

He asked her to come to the after party but she declined, "I'm sorry I am not in the party mood but thank you." He understood and kissed her goodbye.

Nikki and Vinny walked into the Barnes and Noble; she was walking around and went to the spot where she met Luca. Underneath her breath she whispered, "I love you babe." She walked back to the front where Giovanni Gambino, the author of Mulberry to Rome was doing the book signing. She was waiting online when this old lady turned around and said to her, "I wish I had a time machine to go back in time." Nikki couldn't help but smile, that's what she had said to Luca.

She looked at the old lady, "Don't we all."

Nikki had a tiny tear in her eye, she felt Luca; she knew he was there with her. She was next in line when she dropped her book. As she bent down to pick it up she saw D&G shoes staring right at her, and got the chills all down her back. The man bent down to pick up the book with her, "is this yours?" She couldn't believe how the events were just like the day she met Luca. She got up and got really light headed and dizzy. The man held her by her waist so she wouldn't fall back, "are you ok?"

"CUT! CUT! CUT! Clooney, Clooney, Clooney, how many times do I have to tell you that you can't touch my Bianca, where in the script does it say you touch her? Please show me."

George just throws his hands in the air. Nikki turns around, "Luca I changed a few scenes because you refused to remove the part where you die SO I thought it would be ok if George could hold me up like you did that day we met." Nikki looks at George and they both smile at each other. Luca walks over to the both of them; turns to George, "you started like a Lion and ended like an ant!" then turns and gives George his back.

He wraps his arms around Nikki's waist, "Babe you see I knew getting George to play this part would be a bad idea, but I promised you George Clooney and when I make a promise I keep it. You see when you look at him like that, you make my blood boil." He gives Nikki a big long kiss and then turns around and says to George, "no touching!"

George laughs, "Luca I know, I know, she's all yours but it's just a movie."

Luca smiles at George, "Yeah like I said, NO TOUCHING."

They finally finished the movie and Nikki was so proud of her Luca. "I am so proud of you and how you set out to do all you dreamed of doing." Luca grabs her and kisses her, "Babe, I couldn't have done it without you. I knew when I met you that you were the one and now look you are having my kid and starring in my movie. I love you Nikki." He kisses her and then bends over and kisses her belly, "I love you too Francesco."

Nikki smiled, "I have to say I really love that name."

"Babe where is my lucky tie?" Nikki walked over to him with his tie before he could finish his sentence. He smiled at her, "you know me too well." She sat on the bed and admired him as he was getting dressed. Luca looked at himself in the mirror, "you know babe there isn't a mirror I don't like." Nikki couldn't help but smile, "You know Luca I thank my lucky stars everyday that we made it out of the warehouse alive, when I saw you fall to the floor I was sure you were dead." Luca walked over to her, "Babe I knew what was going down you didn't think I was going to be prepared, I'm just glad I had that vest on and plus we gave Mark one hell of a Movie, don't you agree?" Nikki nodded and just tried to change the subject, she didn't like to think about what could've happened. "So what's this meeting about, did they say?"

"It's just a little get together with the five families, I know you will miss me but I promise I will come back to you the minute I finish. I can't stand being away from you more than I have too." He leans over and gives her a big luscious kiss, "I will be back in an hour." She kisses him back, "be careful please."

He looks at her, "you know I always am."

Luca walks in and the men all got up and clapped. Luca is flattered and feels honored. They all walk over to him and say hello.   Luca takes his place next to Vinny and is very happy to see Mr. B there too.

Carlo starts the speech, "Luca what can I say, congratulations. I have to say I was the most sceptical of the bunch. When you pitched us on how we should get into the entertainment business and music business, I thought you were crazy. But now look at us, we got the drugs off our streets, Junior has a record deal and Undercover Secrets is going to hit the theatres in a few months. Who knew that we would do so well?"

Luca is very proud of himself.

Peter, the old man adds to it, "Luca I am so happy that I can actually sleep at night. We are also very happy for you and Nikki; we wish you both the best." They all raised their glasses to towards Luca, "A Salute!"

THE END

ABOUT THE AUTHORS

GIOVANNI GAMBINO & RITA GAMBINO

Author Rita Gambino was born and raised in Brooklyn, New York. She is one of four sisters. Her main priority in life is her kids. The mom of three gets her drive and determination from her kids. Most of her work is inspired by her dreams and through the trials in her life. With hard work and mostly her determination she hopes that she can achieve all her dreams and goals in life. Rita Gambino co-authored with Giovanni Gambino "Destiny".

Giovanni Gambino is the author of Prince of Omerta, Undercover Secrets and Mulberry Street to Rome B.C. He was born in the province of Palermo in Sicily and grew up in Torretta, located in a mountainous area overlooking Palermo. Thirty-seven years old, he is the youngest in a family that includes four sisters and a brother. His family moved to Bensonhurst, a neighbourhood in southwestern Brooklyn in 1985. He grew up in the underworld as the son of Don Francesco "Ciccio" Gambino. Don Ciccio was sentenced to 30 years in federal prison in 1988 and passed January 4th 2012 honorably in prison. Giovanni was raised and cared for by real men of honor, out of respect for Don Ciccio these men of respect taught Giovanni about the real underworld and how to avoid precarious situations. Visit him online at giovannigambino.com